Murder off U Street

An Academic Mom Mystery

Books by Jacque Rosman

The Academic Mom Mystery Series
Book One: Murder in Georgetown
Book Two: Murder off U Street

Coming Soon!
Book Three: Murder at the Waterfront

For more information
visit: www.SpeakingVolumes.us

Murder off U Street

An Academic Mom Mystery

Jacque Rosman

SPEAKING VOLUMES, LLC
NAPLES, FLORIDA
2025

Murder off U Street

Copyright © 2025 by Jacqueline Corcoran

All rights reserved. No part of this book may be reproduced or transmitted in any form or by any means without written permission.

ISBN 979-8-89022-228-2

To Mark, who does so much to support me

Acknowledgments

To Kathryn LeBlanc and Laure Levin, who beta-read drafts and helped me develop this project, as well as smoothed my rougher edges.

Chapter One

Week One
Monday Morning

Returning to work on Mondays after a weekend of tending to our little kids was always a welcome relaxation. And today, performing one of his few regular household duties without being told, my husband, Seth, was ready to do drop off at Beth El Preschool in Alexandria. We'd chosen the school not so much due to religious affiliation but because they took two-year-olds *and* kept them four hours at a shot—one hour more per day than any other preschool in town—*and* did so three times a week instead of a measly two.

But as usual, Mother must orchestrate, so it all came together at the finale: walking out the door. I called out, faking excitement, "Look, Daddy's going to school! Let's get in the car." It's not wrong to be fake when you're doing it for your child, right?

Alyssa, age three, adorable even with a diaper underneath a lavender-colored, flower-sprigged dress, veered toward a weed sprouting in the corner of the garage. "Oh, look—flower!"

Used to her distractibility from the house to the car, I hovered behind, ready to steer her by the shoulders toward the Honda sedan that Seth drove; he found the minivan a touch emasculating.

Morning shenanigans returned anew with the same tired arguments. This was like couples therapy but much worse. Alyssa screwed up her face and flushed. "I need Pink Leopard, show and share."

Cute—they'd changed it from *show and tell* in my day. Now we *shared*. "I'll get it," I said to Seth, who grabbed his phone from the passenger seat.

Looking at the screen, he said, "I have a call at 9:30. I'll email Jeff to prepare him in case I'm late. But I need to get in."

I whirled off and clunked up the stairs in my boots to fetch Pink Leopard. Also, in my day, we named our stuffed animals actual names.

Back at the car, Alyssa accepted Pink Leopard and rubbed his soft fur against her cheek while Noah glared at me from his car seat. He gnawed on his pacifier, his tiny teeth stretching the rubber nipple. He hit the back of his head against his seat, arching his back, and took the pacifier out to wail.

"What's wrong?" I asked.

Noah flexed his ankle toward me, his big toe sticking out as if it had touched an accident from Miffy, our aging Maltese. Ah, a hole had started in the toe of his sock.

"Off," he said. His little sensitivities, like decals of dinosaurs on t-shirts, drove him crazy, as did most socks. Most of all, he didn't like me paying attention to *her*.

Back upstairs, I went to rummage in the top drawer of the dresser Grammy had purchased for his room. I had to give her credit for generosity; she was intent on furnishing both kids' rooms in ways that cost more than we wanted to spend. I fished two pairs of socks, an extra to keep in his Batman backpack.

Returning to the car, my son the emperor, eczema on his cheek inflamed, watched as his servant, me, leaned before him to yank on the new sock. His foot was sturdy with a nice arch, the undersides untouched and smooth. He hadn't walked the rough road yet.

Finally, I stood, my duties complete. "Do you want another hug and kiss goodbye?"

He scowled, "No!" As I backed up, he bellowed, "Don't go!" We did this dance—*go away, don't leave me*—quite a bit.

Seth put his phone down, then moved the car in reverse, and waved. "Bye, Mommy!"

I slammed the car door, averting my eyes from Noah's anguished face. As I waved, my family drove off to a gentle folk song made famous by *Curious George: The Movie.*

* * *

A few minutes later, fast walking like Jason Bourne, I crossed the dirt path from our townhome community around a drainage ditch to the parking lot of the industrial office park with the anchor business of Smoot Lumber (founded in 1858) that housed our "campus." I must have had the shortest commute in the region, save the burgeoning class of teleworkers. Living that close, most people suggested they wouldn't be able to draw the boundary between work and home. However, as an assistant professor with two toddlers and working toward tenure, I was all about efficiency.

I entered the main door of the building that faced Edsall Road and passed the first business, a for-profit medical technology training program. Pulling open the door to "our campus," I strode down the hall of polished tile where my children often raced when the internship director, Rochelle Grunvald, popped out of her office.

"Cara, there you are," she said. "I wanted to catch you before you went into the faculty meeting."

I'd wanted to print off a few student papers to achieve *something* during our two-hour meetings, but resigned, I stopped. Rochelle's office, unlike mine, was colorful with plants, pictures, photos, and the occasional inspirational message. She was definitely a nester.

"We have a problem," she said.

"Somebody got an A minus?" I hazarded.

Rochelle hitched a smile to acknowledge my cheeky comment and went on. "We got a call this morning from the supervisor at Victim Services—" she said, pausing so I could say,"Oh no."

Rochelle knew I'd been the driving force behind the development of this internship at the unit of the D.C. Police Department that worked with victims of crime. "Apparently, Kaitlyn left a message for you, too."

To be honest, I hardly checked my phone; office phones were increasingly like full reception dashboards of old and much too complicated. "Did she email?" To me, that was the way people conducted business. Perhaps things were still old school at the police station.

Rochelle shook her head. "She was complaining about her intern, Emily."

I'd taught Emily Vinter in both her first and second years. She was a top student. That's why I thought she'd be ideal for this placement.

"She was driving around in the middle of the night with a police officer. According to Kaitlyn, Emily's 'involved with' this officer."

"That will happen." When Rochelle's head went back in surprise, I said, hands up, "Not that I condone it. But she's young and attractive. Of course, the police are going to like her."

"The problem is this particular policeman already has a girlfriend. And she's also a police officer at the Metro Police Department."

* * *

While I sat in the faculty meeting, Rochelle arranged a meeting with Emily and me for 1 p.m. before classes started. Emily's shoulders were hunched, and her face looked pale as I passed her and Rochelle on my way to unlock the office.

Inside, I was going for the absent-minded professor look with its usual state of disarray—drafts of papers and books littered the top of the desk. Papers to return were stacked on the floor so they wouldn't get caught up in what I still had to accomplish. Poster board papers covered in highlighter from student in-class activities unfurled from against the wall where I'd shoved them. It just never felt right going straight from class to the recycle bin.

Last time he'd graced the office, my son, Noah, had pulled the books from my shelf and left a brightly striped plastic ball behind. I'd learned that small boys were like dogs—if you threw a ball, they would chase it.

When Rochelle and Emily pulled out the chairs that faced the desk, we were maxed out on space.

Emily had large green eyes, wildly curly hair, and freckles across her nose. Like most of our students, she was young, perhaps a year or two out of undergrad. She was shy, and although she did well on tests and papers, she didn't raise her hand and blushed easily.

"What do you already know about why we've called you in?" I liked to start this way before I went into a lot of unnecessary backstories and explaining.

Emily looked askance at Rochelle, then turned to me. "Ms. Grunvald said that my supervisor made a complaint." She swallowed. "I worked a suicide case. The counselors are always mad about being on-call and having dispatch send them out in the middle of the night. They were kind of resentful that I didn't have to go since I'm a student." She emphasized the word *student*, as I imagined the other counselors did.

"So, how did you happen to be out in the middle of the night and know there was a call to respond to?" Rochelle asked, her face wreathed in pretend concern.

"I was riding around with a patrol officer," Emily said.

I remained silent so she would feel the pressure to fill in. It didn't take long.

"I met him on a ride-along during training." Her face flushed. "I guess we're dating now. You probably already knew that."

When I nodded, she burst out, "But all the Victim Services' counselors are dating police officers. Some of them are even married to them."

"So, there's not a policy?" Policies had sure changed throughout the years. In my day, the student pool was what male professors drew from for their second wives.

"No one said anything about that when I started, but now my supervisor, Kaitlyn, said I'm not allowed to. By the way, she's dating a robbery investigator." Emily's flush deepened.

"What's your boyfriend's name?" I asked.

"I'm not sure I'd call him—I mean, we hadn't got to that—Jack Randolph," she finally said.

"And what's his—situation?" I asked.

"He broke up with his girlfriend. Is that what you mean?"

"That's what he told you?" Rochelle's tone was one of deep suspicion, and her artificial eyebrow was already there.

Emily flushed again. "His ex-girlfriend is a police officer. That's why Kaitlyn is so mad."

Rochelle interjected. "And she doesn't want to lose support for the agency. Victim Services has worked for years to forge a relationship with the police. They don't want to burn bridges. Does that make sense?"

Emily nodded, her eyes filling with tears. Rochelle handed her the tissue box on my desk. That was another thing I talked about with students: not to shove tissue boxes at clients when they're crying; there's an implicit message: clean up your face!

With a balled-up tissue to her face, Emily said, "The suicide on Saturday?" Her mouth trembled. "Her name was Siobhan Weaver." She covered her mouth with her hand.

"That's okay," I said. "This is a confidential conversation." Students weren't supposed to reveal real names of clients.

"I realized—" Emily's voice broke. "I had counseled her before."

Initially, I'd thought Emily was crying because of "being in trouble." Now, I realized she was more upset about the suicide.

"Oh, no. That's awful." Rochelle murmured her sympathy, putting aside the bad-cop routine.

"I'm sorry," Emily said, indicating the tears.

"That's a tough one for anyone," I added and felt fortunate I hadn't had the experience.

"At first, I didn't recognize her. I didn't realize how different someone looks when they're dead." Emily grimaced. "It was about a month ago when we met. I enjoyed talking to her." Her grimace turned to a smile. "Her future seemed, I don't know, bright, by the time I left. She was going to start an MFA program—in creative writing. We had that in common, since I was in grad school, too."

"Was she suicidal then?" Rochelle asked.

People used to be afraid of asking someone directly about suicidal tendencies, worried they might put terrible ideas into a person's head. Now best practice was to ask.

Emily brushed back her hair in earnest. "She said she had thoughts jump into her mind, but she would never follow through. She said she was brought up Catholic, and she hated guns and all the shootings in America."

"Did you do a safety plan?" Rochelle asked.

"For the violence or the suicide?" Emily looked wary as if wondering if she'd done anything wrong.

"Both," Rochelle barked.

"She claimed there was no violence that night. Someone walking by, I guess, heard yelling and screaming, called the police anonymously from a cell phone, and didn't want to get involved other than that."

"So why did the police call in Victim Services?" I asked.

Emily's eyes were wide. "She was so distraught and hysterical, they thought he must have done something to her."

I also knew that a crying woman was hard for police to deal with and that they believed tears were a signal of some deep distress or mental illness that they couldn't contend with.

Emily nodded. "After she calmed down and told me a little bit about what was going on, I found out that she had a therapist and psychiatrist, and I got their names for the report." Emily screwed up her face, remembering. "So, she was getting treatment and was taking an antidepressant. Not sure if she said which one. And hydrozine, something like that."

"Hydroxyzine?" I guessed. The pharmaceutical names all sounded the same. "A cousin of Benadryl, but only available by prescription. Used for all kinds of conditions—insomnia, anxiety, agitation, anger."

"She was also on Gabapentin," Emily said.

"Another one that's widely prescribed now," I said. "Anxiety, bipolar light."

"Bipolar light?" Rochelle chuckled.

"That's what I heard one doctor call it," I said. "Even though the only thing Gabapentin is FDA-approved for is restless leg syndrome."

Rochelle turned toward Emily and smiled for the first time. "Okay, it sounds like you covered your bases. I'm not sure your supervisor would've done anything differently."

Emily didn't smile back. "Maybe if I'd known the right thing to say." She dropped her eyes to the gray carpet.

"There is no right thing to say." I leaned back in my swivel chair, feet flat on the floor, and thought of my children. You can bet that they had fun spinning around on that thing.

"You gave her space to talk and cry," Rochelle said. "A container for her feelings."

"You listened." I felt like part of a Greek chorus. "You were non-judgmental."

"I struggled a bit with that—when she said she was dating a married guy."

I wondered if Emily saw any irony here. She was dating someone who may or may not be involved with someone else.

"She was drinking," Emily said. "I smelled alcohol on her breath, and there was a bottle with about a third of red Sauvignon and two glasses on the coffee table. She was worried what her boyfriend would do if she broke up with him. He'd burned his hand the last time she tried. That seems pretty desperate, right?"

I checked the time on my monitor and peered closer, shocked at how quickly time had gone by. When I was amusing children, we could color, dance, bake cookies, and play Candyland, and only 45 minutes would've passed. "I'm sorry," I said. "This is a terrible time to stop, but I have to pick my children up from preschool."

* * *

I drove into the car-pool line just as the last SUV was being loaded with children. Therefore, I was technically not late. As the preschool director, a barrel-bodied woman who talked constantly, walked Noah and Alyssa down the three steps from the doorway, I leaned forward so they could see me through the window, smiling and waving.

"Hi, Mama," Alyssa said, once ensconced into the driver-side back seat.

I hadn't trained Alyssa to say *Mama*. She had picked up the name from multiple Beauty and the Beast viewings. The little teacup called his mother Mama in it, so she'd adopted this moniker rather than *Mom*.

She thrust a piece of construction paper, stiff with glue, toward me.

"Ooh, glittery." Silver flakes rained down onto the console of the minivan.

"A dreidel."

Still in park, I turned back to her and smiled. "Can I put it on the fridge?"

She nodded. "It's for Hanukkah. Light the lights for Hanukkah!"

We had been celebrating Christmas until now but had vacillated about what to do long-term. "Jewish people do Hanukkah," I said, testing Alyssa out.

"And I'm Jewish," she said emphatically.

"Are you?"

"Yes," she said, very certain.

"All right then." I filed this away to tell Seth.

Noah arched his back in his car seat, his eyebrows pulling down, perturbed. "Where pacie?"

I produced the pacifier, affectionately abbreviated as *pacie*, from my vest pocket. *Voila!*

Noah stuck it into his mouth, and the irritation went down a notch.

"Shall we go to the playground?" I asked as I pulled out into traffic. Many mothers drove off from preschool to put their children down for naps. My kids wouldn't nap and getting them to sleep at night was hard enough, so I saved my efforts until then. But all kids need naps. By late afternoon, they were as unreasonable as drunks.

A few blocks from the school, we circled the Temple to the back of the parking lot, where the playground edged against the woods behind. When we emerged, the sharp air brought tears to my eyes and burned my nose. I hoped the vest, designed for mothers who needed free movement in their arms to carry children, would be warm enough. Noah wore shorts and a sweatshirt as if he'd stepped out of another season entirely.

At the gate, I let the kids bolt through it to the other preschoolers, and I made sure it was latched as it closed behind me. The last thing we needed was escapees.

The regulars were out there, trolling, like me, for company. I'd learned that the kids were easier when they were out of the house rather than inside, and it didn't hurt to have adult company. The usual conversations ensued—naps, potty training, foods children would and would not eat. I ceased to be a working professional, even in my business casual attire rather than the jeans and leggings the other mothers wore. But, in the back of my mind, I replayed the conversation with Rochelle and Emily. I researched on my phone the name of the suicide victim. I couldn't find anything about her death but, then again, news of suicides wasn't typically broadcast.

I would have to call back Kaitlyn, Emily's supervisor, once I was in a quiet place where I wouldn't be interrupted. In the meantime, I would stay with the other mothers as long as the fun lasted, or when one of my children, usually Alyssa, wanted to go home.

Chapter Two

Tuesday Morning

The following day, as I walked across the parking lot from the dirt path, a D.C. Metro police SUV pulled up to the curb next to the entrance of the building that housed the school of social work. Alexandria was only six miles from the D.C. line but an hour in traffic, as my husband complained each day.

Emily slipped out on the passenger side. Ah, the boyfriend, giving her a ride to school. I got a look at the man in question. He was older—perhaps seven to ten years senior to Emily—than I had drawn him in my head, his hair receding in front.

He must have sensed me staring and glared back at me from the driver's side, gunning the engine. Emily turned around, her hand on the glass door of the building, as if she wanted to wave goodbye, but he was already driving away, toward the light to turn left, which would bring him to the I-95 ramp to D.C.

Inside, the tables in my research class were arranged in the "social work circle" so beloved by our instructors. It worried me that all the students were female. Unchecked estrogen did not bode historically well for my teaching evaluations.

Where these students differed was in their ability and motivation for research. A couple of students like Emily "got it"; in fact, knew it before they set foot in the class and had placed out of foundation research. A small proportion were so lost they "didn't even know what questions to ask," as they put it. Their cluelessness made me worry about the future of our profession.

I tried to inject enthusiasm into my voice, like I did with my children. But it was more complicated with the students because they wouldn't meet you halfway. "Hey, just to get us started, let's go around the room and see where everybody is with their projects," I said. "That'll help me figure out what we should focus on today." I also hoped it would galvanize their efforts.

"Let's see, I'll start here." I looked at the strawberry-blonde to my left with a diamond nostril ring. "Maddy?"

She straightened. At least the prompt had caused her to emerge from an inward reverie.

"Cara?" Despite her glasses, Birkenstocks, and frizzy hair, Naomi often spoke for the other students. "Can we meet with our groups first to catch up on where we are?"

At least she gave me something to work with, so I gave them seven minutes to talk. Emily caught my eye as the other students chatted in groups of four. She was the only person to work alone on her research project. This was partly because the police department wouldn't let someone from the outside, another student, come in to collect data. Also, Emily was the only person in the class who could carry it off alone. But I also detected tension between her and the others that perhaps went beyond the project groupings. Some of that was possibly because of her field placement in what some students saw as a "white supremacist structure," and they associated her with it.

A contemporary movement in social work was "abolitionism," which was for abolishing the criminal justice and child welfare systems since they involved more people of color than the numbers in the population warranted. While there were other positions on how reforms could be made, abolitionism was at the more radical end, and thus, our Masters' students loved it. Perhaps that explained the attitude they carried toward Emily.

Emily made her way to the front of the classroom where I stood. The table I was using for my stuff was already scattered with papers. How had I been able to make a mess in such a short time? Alyssa came by her messy room honestly.

"How are you doing?" I asked.

Emily's face was pale again, freckles smudging her skin under the fluorescent lighting and her eyes red-rimmed. She glanced about as if to make sure no one was listening. The other students were enrapt in conversation, probably complaining about the class and its requirements.

"I'm having a hard time sleeping," Emily admitted.

"That would be pretty common after what you went through, but not getting enough sleep makes you feel terrible."

She nodded. "It really started before. That was why I was riding around with Jack in the middle of the night. I couldn't sleep. Anyway—"

She flapped her hand, dismissing the personal talk. "I just wanted to let you know before I present where I am with the project. The IT guy, Ethan, is still giving me a hard time about my data request. He says he needs it in writing from the deputy assistant chief, and Anita, the executive director, said she submitted the request. Kaitlyn doesn't want me to keep bothering her about it. She said she'd deal with Anita directly. I feel like I'm getting the runaround."

In life, most of the time, you're urged to be an optimist. In research, it's the opposite. Things always go wrong; data agreed upon is never collected; recording devices don't work; the electronic data is lost due to a glitch; people have to give permission for this and that and don't get back to you.

"Can we just print off the reports and use those?" Emily asked. "I know how to do that."

I decided to use this as a teaching moment. "And what's the name of a sampling method for choosing cases you can easily get?"

She smiled, seeing my setup. "A convenience sample. I guess that might not represent the population of women who reported family violence. But can't we just print out all the family violence cases from the year before?"

"What kind of sampling is that when you take all the existing cases?"

Most students couldn't answer that question, but she did quickly. "Population?"

"Correct, but first, we have to cross-reference the Victim Services logs to see which ones had crisis intervention services. We can take all those cases—we're oversampling—because they probably represent a small proportion of total family violence calls. Then, we'll take an equal number, randomly selecting, from the non-Victim Services cases. It's going to involve thousands of cases. And we'll need to link the victim names back up and see if they had repeat calls over the next year. It would be a nightmare to do it by hand."

"What if you miss something important that way?" she asked.

"Good question, but you should have considered the important variables in your conceptualization and justified them. If anything is going on with your data, you'd theoretically find it." I glanced at the other students in their small knots. Gone was the urgency about research projects. "You're not supposed to go on a 'fishing expedition' is what it's called." I turned from one metaphor to another one and said, "I better corral the rest of them." I straightened to raise my voice to get their attention and I realized Emily hadn't made a move to return to her seat. Assuming she needed more direction on her report to the class, I said in a low voice, "It doesn't have to be long. Just how you told me."

She hesitated. "It's not that. I—I'm just not sure Siobhan's death was a suicide. I think it was murder."

* * *

After the research class ended, Emily accompanied me to my office at my direction.

"Okay, so what evidence makes you think it's murder?" I got right to the point as I opened the door with the key. One, I didn't have much time before I returned to my babysitter, Rosa, and two, I was curious. Wasn't Emily in enough trouble for working the suicide and dating a police officer?

She took a deep breath before starting in. "Siobhan told me she wasn't suicidal."

Before speaking, I gestured at a seat as I walked to the chair behind my desk. "At the time you saw her, yes. But that could have changed, depending on her circumstances and mindset." I sat and wheeled my chair up to the desk so I could lean on it.

"But she had such strong beliefs against it—her religion."

"It didn't sound like she practiced her religion." I didn't use the phrase lapsed Catholic, which had a vaguely pejorative air about it. "And people aren't in their right minds when they do this. It could have been an impulse."

"She shot herself in the chest." Emily swallowed. "There was a lot of blood."

I winced. It was a testament to why Emily shouldn't have worked this case without approval. Kaitlyn could easily argue that they wanted to protect the students from getting in over their heads. But there was no point in saying a *told-you-so* now.

Emily put her hand up to her chest over her sweatshirt. "That's the way that women shoot themselves."

"Where did you learn that?" Everyone knew that completed suicides were higher in men, although women made more attempts. Males used firearms rather than less lethal methods. But I hadn't read this fact.

Emily flushed and ducked her head. "The officer I was with."

I wondered whether it was because women were feeling "heartbreak" when they felt suicidal. Gruesome. And painful. "I know it's not the first choice of women generally, but women do use guns to shoot themselves."

"It's just that she said she hated guns. And this one had its serial number shaved off. That means it was bought on the black market." Emily leaned forward earnestly.

"Maybe her boyfriend got it for her." I made a face. "He sounded like a straight-up fellow."

"But that means he also could have used it on her. It was a toxic relationship, and he wouldn't let her go." Emily went on with her argument. "You know how often women die because of their intimate partner. Maybe she'd broken up with him again. Isn't that the danger point in these types of relationships?"

"Was there prior violence?" When she hesitated, I said, "Come on, I know you looked them up." Looking up clients online raised some ethical concerns, but I wondered how those extended to the matter of police records. Emily had to document in the report that she worked with this woman. It would be easy to run her name through and her boyfriend's.

"Nothing on her," she said. "And she wouldn't give his full name to the police or me, but when she was talking, she called him 'Zach.'" I nodded, taking the information in. Zachary was a popular name now for the preschool set.

"Did she write a note?" I asked.

"Supposedly."

I quirked an eyebrow. "That would be evidence for a suicide."

"I don't know what it said. He wouldn't let me read it."

The *he* must have been her Jack again. She was leery about using his name too often.

"I saw it in his hand. A piece of paper ripped out of a spiral notebook. But I also saw a notebook on the nightstand. When I leafed through it, a page was torn out, but the writing was on the pages afterward."

I cocked my head, not getting it. "What did that mean to you?"

"Maybe she'd written about feeling that bad in the past, but it wasn't a new entry. Maybe her boyfriend read her diary before and knew he could find something that read like a suicide note and tore it out."

I shrugged. There was so much supposition here, I didn't know where to start. "You said your—Officer Randolph." I reverted to the official title. "Didn't want you to look at the suicide note, yet you saw her dead body and wandered around the crime scene?" I wanted to be more sarcastic. *That's where he drew the line?*

"He said he didn't want me getting any ideas." She flushed, and I didn't want to embarrass her further by prying into what that meant. Emily held up her left hand. "I knew from her printing she was left-handed. We have that type of printing—it leans back because your hand covers up the writing as you go. But when I asked Jack what hand she'd used to shoot, he said her right." She saw the question on my face and shook her head. "I wanted to see what he would say."

"A gun is kind of heavy," she continued. "Wouldn't someone use their dominant hand?"

"My son is left-handed but throws and kicks with his right," I offered.

"Hmm, that's interesting." She looked away in the direction of the spilled books, as if thinking.

"You don't want it to be suicide." I had learned to go for the underlying meaning.

She turned back and held my eye contact. "It's sad that a beautiful and smart young woman would want to kill herself, but I don't think it was that."

"Are you sure you're not over-identifying?" I asked.

"You mean like countertransference?" she asked. When I nodded, Emily replied, "Maybe a little, but that's not always a bad thing if you're aware of it, right?"

"It's something to talk about in supervision, for sure." However, I recognized that, at this point, she and Kaitlyn didn't even meet the hour a week they were supposed to.

Emily smiled as if trying to make light of things. "At least I finally had something to write about in my process recordings for Clinical Practice."

Process recordings were unique to social work education. Students would recount a meaningful interaction with a client, using the dialogue at the time, and then analyze the moment-to-moment interaction in terms of the theories and skills they were learning in coursework. Because Emily had been in my first-year foundation practice class, she knew that I heavily relied on them.

"How did you even get a chance to work a case?" That was one of the major problems at this placement, among others: Emily wasn't getting an opportunity to practice and apply what she learned in coursework.

"I asked one of the counselors if I could go out with her on an evening shift. She knew the officers who called for Victim Services and just wanted a chance to kick back with them. I was happy to finally get a chance."

"Okay, that's great." Sitting back in my chair, I realized that in my conversation with her, I might have been encouraging her to go rogue and alienate herself further from the police department. That we didn't need, so I asked, "Emily, what is the role of the Victim Services worker?"

She was surprised at what must have seemed a trick question. "To see victims, to help them deal with the after-effects of crimes."

"Do you see what I'm getting at? Your role isn't investigator." I felt a bit hypocritical saying this after the case I'd solved last year.

"Aren't we supposed to advocate for clients?"

I kept my face impassive, waiting to see where the argument would take her.

"I want to see justice for her," Emily said. "And what if the person who killed Siobhan kills again?"

Chapter Three

Tuesday Evening

I felt as emotionally exhausted as a scarecrow seeping straw when I descended from the nighttime routine. I plopped down on the couch next to Seth, who was doomscrolling to "relax." Nothing would put the stuffing back inside me at this point except waking up to a whole new day. But I wanted some time to myself, even with the awareness that Noah could easily appear at five-thirty the following day.

We tried showing him the clock and saying, "Only come in when it says seven." He listened intently, sucking with force on the pacifier. But every morning between five and six, he climbed into my side of the bed in his briefs. Early on in life, he'd shucked the PJs. Non-Greeks, Seth and I had given birth to a frat boy.

I glanced over at Seth on the couch next to me. "Remember, I have to leave by seven tomorrow."

Seth raised his head from his phone. "I have an emergency meeting with the defense attorneys at nine. It was just scheduled at the end of the day."

"I have to go to Richmond tomorrow. You know this."

"Do you have to?" he had the nerve to ask.

I stared at him in astonishment. "You know I have a job, right?"

"You never had to do one of these before," he pointed out.

"There's a new dean in town." I preferred the one-pagers that our previous deans had used to summarize our accomplishments in perfunctory yet strengths-based terms. "He claims that people were begging for proper evaluations, and now he is very proud of himself for doing them." Some people, I guess, always wanted feedback, and by feedback, I mean to be told that they were brilliant and wonderful. I just wanted to be left alone to get on with my work.

"Can we get Rosa to come in the morning?" Seth asked.

"That's when she works at the gym childcare." I stiffened. "And you know she doesn't drive."

"She could just stay here with them."

"All day? You want them to sit around here and watch TV? Come on, work with me here. Just leave right before eight-thirty. The preschool staff will take them at eight-forty-five, especially if it's a man doing drop off. Scootch into work from there."

"That's leaving it too tight. Traffic's too heavy by then."

"Just say your wife has a meeting, and you had to take the kids to preschool. They'll think you're a hero."

"Then I'll have to turn around and get them at one."

I tried to remind myself that Seth became grouchy when tired, and this wasn't his most authentic self. "You do realize," I said, jaw tight. "That's what I do every day."

He stomped off shortly after to bed, the best place for him, and I was left with my me-time, eroded now by guilt. Then I was mad that I felt guilty.

* * *

In the morning, I dressed in my mommy *uniform*—a long skirt over leggings and a sweater over a long-sleeve t-shirt. When I returned later, I could transform from professional to mother by pulling off the boots and, *voila,* whipping off the skirt.

In the meantime, Seth was supposed to feed the kids breakfast. But when I came downstairs, Seth, a champ of executive functioning in making travel and wedding arrangements, was suddenly in a dither. "Noah just wanted a bagel with butter."

Noah looked up at me from the table, his little teeth gnawing at the over-processed, grocery-store bagel, a staple for his diet. It was soaked in butter.

"He has to have protein," I announced. Meltdowns over imagined slights would ensue otherwise. It felt wrong to cook pork before the kids went to their Jewish preschool, but it was the only thing they both liked. Between bacon in the morning and Alyssa's pepperoni slices for her after-school snack, we were making a muck of it. Frying bacon is not a five-minute affair, and by the time I had it cooked crispy like he wanted, I was pushing up against the absolute last leaving time for Richmond. I kissed both kids goodbye on the tops of their heads to avoid their bacon-greased fingers staining my clothes. I turned away so I couldn't see Noah's little face of distress, only hear his screams of abandonment. Alyssa, munching on bacon, seemed to have attained object permanence. But Noah was still too young. I was honored to be that needed. I felt mean turning away, but I told myself that he had to get used to *self-soothing*—a popular term among parents these days. At the same time, I was well-versed in attachment theory. Noah hardly knew yet that he was a person aside from me.

Outside, I started the car and glanced up at the front window. Seth had moved in to distract or comfort him, and Noah was not fighting the blinds to find me. I put the gear into reverse and backed away.

During the drive, I appreciated the fact that the highway was not cluttered by billboards and industrial buildings that backed up to the frontage road, as they had in Texas, where Seth and I met. I enjoyed the white noise of wheels against the road rather than the high volume of toddlers boxing my ears. The scenic highlight of the drive was the sparkling water of the Rappahannock River that passed under I-95.

With that, I was transported to the American South, where oak trees gave way to pines, the temperature warmed five degrees, and the politics became more conservative.

When I reached the Richmond campus, then circled and jammed myself into a spot, it was my exact meeting time with the dean. I jutted into the road but didn't have time to fool with perfecting my parallel parking. The "quickie" automatic parking meter rejected my credit card repeatedly for no good reason, so I dug out an alternative card it liked better.

I shoved the ticket onto the dashboard, slammed and locked the minivan, and began running in high-heeled boots, my laptop banging against my leg in the tote I carried, which was a diaper bag and briefcase in one. I would have some nice bruises on my leg at the end of this venture.

Then, I faced the "eco-friendly elevators," meaning they were slow to come and even slower to rise. I was only three minutes late when I got to the dean's office. Breathless, I asked for him at the secretary's desk.

"Hi Cara, good to see you. He's just finishing his last appointment. You can relax," she said, smiling. Although our deans constantly turned over, Pam, the dean's secretary with the always-trendy hairstyles, was the one constant.

A person I didn't recognize emerged from Dean Bingham's office. He'd hired a slate of staff to complete his bureaucracy, and staff now outnumbered the faculty. Despite the ratio, we had to do all our own secretarial work.

Bingham smiled in a way that struck me as lacking in sincerity and gestured grandly for me to "Come in, Cara, have a seat." I hadn't been in the dean's office since the school had moved into the floor of a new building during the summer. He hadn't skimped. Light wood, contemporary artwork, and a couple of bright chairs, including a green chaise lounge. An interior decorator had figured out this scheme. Was this still a school of social work? I was used to teaching in abandoned apartment buildings and basements, industrial complexes, and places with water stains on the ceilings. We had gone corporate.

He leaned back, appearing very comfortable behind his desk rather than meeting with me in the sitting room section of the office. "I wanted to start with the personnel committee's third-year review report on your case for tenure and promotion."

I nodded.

"In all, your record of scholarship is very strong. Everyone agrees on that."

"Thank you." I tucked my hair behind my ear modestly.

"As you know, a candidate should score *excellent* in two areas and *very good* in the third. So, your colleagues rated you *excellent* there, but what's going on with your teaching evaluations?" He straightened and picked up the sole piece of paper from the glass surface of his desk. He didn't have bookshelves—only a couple of bland abstract metal pieces. He had no apparent interest in being an academic and having a research agenda or publishing. His plan all along was to become a dean and run the place. We had all been taken in by his charming presentation and articulate job talk during his interview. He had memorized all our names, roles at the school, and areas of interest.

My eye contact stayed steady as I explained that students needed to be held to a graduate student standard, and they were, after all, planning to work with vulnerable people. I tried to encourage questions and extra help. I gave out mid-semester evaluations, trying to strain off some of the vitriol from the end-of-the-semester ones when they were anonymously completed. Of course, the students had input on what would help them learn, but it wasn't a democracy.

"And you know how social work students feel about research," I concluded.

"You forget that's what I taught as well." Like I was supposed to track his career path as well as my own. "And there are ways to do it, so they'll admit it's fair. It just takes a lot of time." He leaned back again in his chair and smoothed his tie. "Just relying on the quantitative scores, your teaching evaluations overall, work out to a 'C.'" He smiled, but it wasn't friendly. "You know a 'C' is a failure in graduate school."

He'd invested considerable effort in calculating this across classes; this wasn't an automatic University process. He seemed to have a vendetta against me, and I couldn't fathom why. Most deans celebrated faculty members who published as prolifically as I did.

He went on. "You know what the average teaching evaluation is for our instructors?"

"Are you including both full-time faculty and adjuncts?"

"Both." He named an unlikely figure.

I attempted a logical argument. "Given that adjuncts teach seventy-five percent of our courses, it's in their best interest to secure favorable student evals to keep their positions. The simplest way to achieve those criteria is to give all A's."

I recalled the research findings, feeling hot and prickly with the long-sleeved shirt and sweater. "They've done studies. Male and female instructors are held to different standards. They analyzed Rate My Professor, and women were predominantly judged on traits like being organized and 'nice.'" My fingers hooked into air quotes. "Men weren't evaluated based on those criteria."

Dean Bingham's lips maintained their mocking curl as if my reliance on research was a sign of desperation. Nevertheless, I continued. "I'm sure you're aware of the study where they offered an online course with blinded instructor names. A man supposedly taught one and the other by a woman. It turned out that the course believed to be taught by a man received higher ratings."

Seemingly unimpressed, he studied his notes. "'Instructor doesn't give feedback,'" he read.

"I grade papers within a week." That was at least a week sooner than anyone else; some instructors never returned papers. Students didn't mind too much if they got A's. "I do provide feedback," I went on, allowing myself a faint smile. "Sometimes, perhaps too much. I get caught up in editing. When I realize it, I mark the spot and suggest, 'Take it from here,' then I try to stick with the bigger picture."

When he opened his mouth, I cut him off, needing to defend myself. "Now, it may not always be the feedback they want to hear," I admitted. "Maybe that's what they're reacting to."

When grading, I adhered to the feedback sandwich approach. I started with a compliment. *This is an interesting topic/case*, or *Wow, you have some challenging clients at your field placement!* Or, *Sounds like you're getting great experience!* Those exclamation points were intended to soften the blow for the constructive criticism that followed, the ham in the sandwich, so to speak, before closing with another positive note.

He pointed at his notes. "What's this policy about waiting twenty-four hours to ask questions after receiving a grade?" He had meticulously reviewed all my materials, searching for any errors or oversights, and had taken notes.

I forced a chuckle. "I borrowed that policy from my three-year-old's soccer coach. He advises parents to take a twenty-four-hour cool-off before emailing him about the way their child was treated or why they didn't get to play more."

Dean Bingham interlocked his fingers and appraised me. Wheeling his chair toward his desk, he said, "Tell you what—go for help—the Center of Teaching and Learning. I can introduce you to the director by email."

Admonishments were unfamiliar to me in academia, whether as a student or instructor. With five years of teaching experience, three in Texas and two here, the idea of needing remedial assistance was disheartening.

Lost in my despondency, I missed some of his ongoing monologue but noted the moue of pride on his lips at his own eloquence. Now, he was going on about my community service. "Your colleagues rated you *very good*, but I thought that was high."

"They gave me credit for the case I solved last year."

He gave me a reproachful look. "Come on, that's not what we do. There's no clear rationale."

"The point was to help an undocumented, marginalized woman who was unjustly accused." Sweat trickled under my cotton undershirt. The two layers were too much, especially with the heat of the rebukes.

"Besides, you were skirting some ethical lines."

Wow, he had a comeback for everything, and it all ended on a negative note for me.

I tried not to show fear. "Whatever brings positive attention to the school, right?"

"Well, we haven't seen any donors open their wallets." He rubbed his fingers together. "If that's what you're asking."

I shrugged. It was his prerogative to not leverage my success and the free publicity it brought. But why wouldn't he?

He went on a similar vein. "In other words, both your community service and your teaching need to be bolstered."

"But the main metric is publications."

"Not among this faculty." He smirked.

I swallowed, feeling sick. He was trying to block my getting tenure, and I couldn't understand why. His eyes crinkled at the corners. It was a tell when he was being phony.

"There's another matter I wanted to discuss," he said.

Flushed, I nodded. Now what?

"As you know, George Mason started their MSW program a couple of years ago. The state legislature doesn't want to support two programs in the same area. The University administration has to take a hard look, and we might have to close the off-campus program. The rent is too high there. The provost said we're in the red."

The provost was the University President's tough guy these days.

"I wanted to tell you in advance because you're one of the people it will affect." He lowered his voice. "But I'll have to trust you to keep it confidential for now."

I couldn't always read the political undertones. Was he telling me in advance to perhaps get another job?

"All of you who are tenured and on the tenure track, you'll be welcome to come to Richmond to teach."

Seth and I had chosen the townhome because it rested on the foothills of the parking lot. Now I would have to commute two hours there and back?

"What about the administrators?" That meant Adam Schwartz, the Director of the off-campus program, and Rochelle, the Director of Internships.

"They were about to retire, anyway. Look, we have a long time frame on this." He stood and straightened his tie. "I just wanted you to be in the know."

Chapter Four

Wednesday Afternoon

Since I'd jumped on the appointment that Kaitlyn, Emily's supervisor, had offered, I had to rush back, past Alexandria where we lived, to D. C. I ruminated on the way—which, according to research, is the worst coping mechanism.

Yes, my evaluations had gone down over time, even as I performed the whole lot of strategies: case-based learning, team-based learning, opportunities for feedback, offering individual meetings, and doing a mid-semester assessment of student opinion to stave off the worst of the ire. Gradually, students had transformed into consumers, with the evaluation the customer satisfaction scale. The students couldn't be blamed for how much college cost. Nothing was worth the price they paid, and they took it out on their instructors. They were paying for A's, and by golly, they would get them. And I was teaching research, a topic that didn't capture their interest. You shouldn't have to work that hard when you're a consumer.

When I pushed open the double doors of the police department thirty minutes later, Emily pounced on me at the entrance. I hadn't seen her waiting through the tinted glass.

"Thanks for coming. Kaitlyn wants to meet with you first." She bit her lip. "I think I'll be fired. I feel sick."

Her skin looked pale and washed out, but I'm sure I looked the same under the fluorescent lighting. "How can you be fired if you're not being paid?" I smiled to see if I could loosen her up before the meeting. It didn't, so I tried reassurance. "That's not the way it usually works.

We'll make an improvement plan first. I'll talk to her. And after that, we should all meet to sort things out."

Emily swallowed and nodded. As she led me to the Victim Services unit on the first floor and walled off behind another glass door, she said, "One good thing . . . I might've found something interesting in the data."

"You got access to the data?" Things were going so badly at the placement that I'd expected this to be a bust as well.

"I can tell you about it later," she replied, glancing at the receptionist with hard cat-eye liner scowling at the front desk. "She's here for Kaitlyn," Emily said to the receptionist. "From my school."

"We'll talk later after I meet with her, okay?" I said to Emily, who nodded and disappeared down the warren of sectional furniture. Kaitlyn's and my conversation would not be strictly private, then. If she wanted to, Emily could position herself to hear.

Kaitlyn was taller and younger than I'd expected. Emily had described a middle-aged busybody, but this woman looked to be in her mid-thirties.

"I'm so sorry I couldn't meet before this," she said as we exchanged a handshake that was heavy on the fingers. At least she didn't have rings to bite into my flesh.

"You saw the news about that Walmart shooting in North Carolina?" she asked, leaning forward confidentially.

"Yes, of course," I said and followed her into the cubicle behind the receptionist, a few feet. "Terrible."

I was used to small spaces—or camping out in other people's offices—to do my social work jobs. It was often like this, but as a result, we were almost knee-to-knee as she sat in a wheeling chair, and I squeezed into molded plastic.

Politeness dictated that I ask about Kaitlyn's work at the latest shooting, but based on Emily's description of her, Kaitlyn was likely to launch off on that topic, and we might not get to the subject at hand: Emily.

"I know you called on Monday," I started with.

"Yes, and I'm sorry I couldn't talk when you called back. We got the news about the shooting, and we had to gear up for it." She paused as if wanting me to pursue the topic.

I would not. "How have things been going since then with Emily?"

"I'm sorry to say, worse." She gripped the edge of the desk and pulled the chair which rolled across some plastic to protect the dingy carpet. "We've worked very hard to establish ourselves with the police. We show them we can make their jobs easier while we tend to the victims and their needs. And it's cost-effective for us to be here. We cost less than sending out multiple units and taking supervisor time."

That was what the research project was supposed to be about. Kaitlyn didn't know if it was cost-effective at this point. She didn't know if it reduced police calls to the same victim. That was the precise question we were trying to answer with the research.

"But a cardinal rule is we don't interfere in police investigations. That suicide she worked—now she's decided it's homicide." Kaitlyn pursed her lips. "Emily should never have been out at that scene."

"Did you talk to the officer that brought her there?" I wanted to make the point that Officer Randolph was implicated here, not just Emily.

"We warn the girls when they start here that the guys are going to come on to them."

Police departments were notoriously male. Only twelve percent of sworn officers in the U.S. were female. "So, the onus is on the intern?"

"Absolutely," Kaitlyn said earnestly and swiped her hair behind her ears. "You can see she doesn't have the maturity to handle a placement like this. She had the gall to approach the investigator Sergeant Bronson on the Siobhan Weaver case. He came stomping in here, mad as heck, demanding a meeting with me and Anita." Kaitlyn made a pained face. "I'm sorry, Emily has to go. We can't let her destroy what we've worked to build for years."

Whoa. Students often catastrophize about failing, when almost no one does. "Usually, we put students on a remedial plan first, give them a chance to improve," I said. "We want this to be a learning experience."

"We've just got too much going on here to babysit someone with problems." She ran her hand through her hair. "This week, a couple of us were out for North Carolina. Next week, I have to go to Rhode Island for the memorial of that mass school shooting."

"I'm sorry, I thought you only dealt with the D.C. area?" What on earth were they doing running around the country? They weren't a national organization, and didn't D.C. have enough crime to deal with?

"We're the experts." Her moue of self-importance was too much like the one I'd seen on Dean Bingham's face earlier. "People look to us and what we're doing. It gives us more exposure for our program when we can help in other parts of the country."

Bells on the front door that I hadn't registered before jangled as if someone had forced it open.

Kaitlyn looked up at the noise and half rose in her chair. "Sorry, I'm wondering if our receptionist—"

A tall man towered over the sectional furniture. "Are you the one from the college?" He spoke to me in a deep, authoritative voice.

Kaitlyn's mouth stretched into a smile that exposed teeth and a lot of gum as the man, a badge on his belt, filled the doorway. "Oh, Sergeant Bronson. This is Dr. Cara Knight."

"Hi, I'm from Virginia University, the School of Social Work." I stood, clutching my notebook, but losing my pen in the process. His bulk took up the remaining space of the modular office. The pen could wait.

"What are you all thinking, sending a student like that over here?"

I was sure Emily could hear his booming voice from whatever little space was allotted to students.

Kaitlyn put a hand on his arm. "Is the conference room in Homicide available?"

"Sure." He hitched a thumb.

I flashed Kaitlyn a grateful look for the suggestion as we filed out of Victim Services to a suite marked Homicide, same floor, but on the other end of the building. He swung open the glass door for us, then stomped ahead, forgetting his manners as he plopped down in one of the chairs. The fluorescent light shining on the table showed greasy fingerprints. *Note to self: Do not touch the table.* I remembered when I'd come down here last year with the kids and the agony of watching them paw all the dirty surfaces. I also remembered Barbara, my mother-in-law, the germaphobe, screaming in my ear afterward on the phone, *Did you wash their hands?*

Sergeant Bronson had a solid college ring on his middle finger. No wedding ring, which didn't surprise me. The police were like a paramilitary operation with some of the same values and traditions. It was important to be married in this culture, but divorce was unfortunately also an outcome.

"I've been working here twenty years, and no civilian tells me what to do, let alone some little intern."

His volume was as high as Noah's, and I wanted to tell him, *Inside voices, please*. I could hardly imagine Emily telling him how to do his job. She barely spoke up in class.

"Can you tell me what happened?" I kept my own voice low and steady. I tried not to let him scare me, but he was intimidating, which I guess was useful for interrogating suspects.

"Sure, I'll tell you what happened. She came marching into Homicide yesterday morning. I was busy as shit as it was. Please excuse my language." This was directed as an aside at me.

I didn't react, disliking that turn of phrase. Don't swear in the first place, or don't be apologetic about it. The fake manners and inherent sexism grated on me.

"At first, I didn't even know who the hell she was. Then she started in on her questions." His mustache, reddish blonde, wagged when he spoke. "First, she asks if I was sure it was a suicide. Okay, some families have a hard time believing that." He turned toward Kaitlyn. "Denial, right?"

When she nodded like he was a good pupil, he went on. "Then she brought up the gun. She said she'd worked with the vic before, who was anti-gun." He shook his head at the very idea. "I told her maybe the vic borrowed or bought it off someone just to off herself. Then she made a big deal about the vic being left-handed. At that point, I said, 'Do you know how many people I've seen blow their brains out?'"

He was going for the shock value, so I had to come back with, "But this woman shot herself in the chest, not the head, right?"

Police weren't supposed to threaten violence anymore to get a confession, but I could see this guy using his bulk and voice to intimidate a suspect. "Yup," he said. "Seen those before, too. The shot was with the right, maybe, but hard to tell for sure. Plus, she'd been drinking.

She had coke in her system, weed. She might have been pretty impaired at that point, just waving the gun around."

Kaitlyn nodded like she could see it.

He leaned toward us and grinned. "The coke surprised her though. The vic wasn't the little miss innocent angel she seemed to think she was." He smacked the table and pushed himself to the back of his chair. "But then she asked if I was going to interview the neighbors." He looked from one to the other of us in outrage. Kaitlyn gave him the dismayed head-shaking he wanted. "You know how many open cases I have?" He jabbed a finger at the table. "This one is open and shut. Finally, I asked her, 'Does your *boyfriend* know you're in here questioning me?' Lord knows why he's dating her." He shook his head. "From what I remember, Randolph was dating a nice-looking lady, a cop, a twin, no less." That thought made him smile. But his outrage took over once again. "Then basically, she tells me that she thought he was acting suspicious, too."

I looked over at Kaitlyn to see if she would share my surprise, but she was hanging on Sergeant Bronson's words as he went on. "She said that he got a phone call right before they headed over to the scene. He claimed it was a C.I."

Kaitlyn turned to me. "That means confidential informant."

"I know," I answered. Her self-important attitude was really starting to grate on me. Emily had been more than fair in her descriptions of Kaitlyn.

As if he hadn't registered our exchange, Sergeant Bronson said, "He told her the call came from his monitor. So what?" Police had those big old monitors in their patrol cars now, so they could follow radio traffic, pull up records, and write their reports. "I mean, the girl's paranoid. Something really wrong there."

"She had worked with the young woman who died before," I said, picturing the scene. When they pulled up, Emily would have recognized the building and probably insisted on going in. What she had seen was worse-case scenario.

"Yeah, yeah, I heard that. She said the officer hustled her out, and she found that suspicious, too."

He gaped at Kaitlyn, who murmured, "Inappropriate."

"Yeah, inappropriate. I would call it crazy. Because then—get this—she spied on him through the blinds." He waved his hand.

"What did she see?" I asked.

He widened his eyes at Kaitlyn, who cleared her throat and shifted her position in her chair. "I think the main point is that Emily wasn't fit for the internship here."

"That may be, but when I talk to Emily, I want to make sure I know what exactly went on." I straightened, alert for the answer. Of course, that wasn't the truth. I wanted to find out what she'd said. I felt terrible. She was in a confessing mood that day after research, and I had become official, reminding her of her role. She might have told me about her suspicions of Jack Randolph if I hadn't shut her down. Maybe if I had listened, that would have changed her fate.

"Nothing went on." Sergeant Bronson grimaced. "That's the point." He twirled his finger in a cliched gesture of madness at his temple.

"Well, what was it that she said? I want to get a sense of her reality-testing."

My excuse seemed to work, and Kaitlyn nodded her agreement.

Sergeant Bronson sighed. "That he was running around, talking on the phone, that back-up took an hour to get there."

"That can be checked, surely," I said to Kaitlyn.

Sergeant Bronson pushed his chair out and stabbed a sausage finger onto the table. "The point is, we would never do that. It was his scene."

When we got Sergeant Bronson calmed sufficiently—his schedule didn't seem that busy if he could allow for these tantrums—Kaitlyn and I walked back to Victim Services. "What kind of notice did you have in mind for Emily?" I asked.

"Oh, it's got to be immediate. You heard him."

Oh, boy, did I. "Can I talk to her first, and then we can meet together?" One thing social workers get used to is delivering bad news. "Where is she?"

"Just keep walking back. You'll see the copier. Her desk is right next to it."

I found the copier and even a printer, but no Emily. I did, however, see her backpack, a scuffed dull maroon. I recognized it from the day Emily was in my office with Rochelle. She must still have been in the building if her backpack was here. She wouldn't have left with an officer to go on a call with an impending dismissal. But had she called Jack Randolph, and he had scooped her away to comfort her?

I grabbed the backpack by the handles and found it surprisingly heavy with the heft of a computer inside. My anxiety spiked. No one would leave their laptop unattended if they were gone for any length of time. Even at a police department. Even in Victim Services.

Back at the front, the receptionist had returned to the front desk. "Hi," I said. "Did you see the intern, Emily, go by?"

Her eyes rolled as if to say, *I can't keep track of everybody.* Instead, she said. "The counselors are supposed to sign themselves out." She glared at a whiteboard where names were written down on the left-hand side. Following her gaze, I saw Emily's name at the bottom, and it had IN checked off.

"She must be here somewhere," she said, stalking out on high heels to wipe the whiteboard where Kaitlyn had marked herself "out." The receptionist sighed, presumably because no one properly signed themselves in and out.

I left the Victim Services suite, ventured into the police department proper, checked the bathroom, and then took the elevator to the basement, where I remembered vending machines. Maybe she went to buy herself some calming caffeine. Late afternoon now, the area was deserted.

The bells jingled as I opened the door to Victim Services again. The receptionist threw me a dirty look. "You're still here?"

"Is she back?" I asked.

"Is who back?"

"The intern, Emily."

She sighed. "I told you, I haven't seen her."

"Can I check again?" I asked.

"Go right ahead."

Kaitlyn was still on the phone in her cubicle, and Emily was not in back. I peered in the sectional offices, the gaps like those from the doors in toilet stalls. It seemed that she must have left the building. If that were the case, she would need her backpack. She wouldn't want to come slinking back in to get it. The nice thing about being ignored was that I could do what I wanted. I hoisted up the backpack. I would let Emily know I had it once I got on the road. I didn't want to get trapped in rush-hour traffic on the way home, something my husband complained about daily.

Chapter Five

Wednesday Afternoon

Delayed at another Constitution Avenue light, I emailed Emily on my phone: *Hey, looked for you at p.d. Please call when you get this. I have your backpack and can bring it to you.*

I stared at the screen, willing a response, until a horn blared behind me. I put my hand up in acknowledgment to the car behind me. At the next light, when there was still no message, I dialed our program director, Adam, who immediately picked up.

After I described the situation, he gave me Emily's phone number and address. "Tell her you'll be there to meet with Rochelle and plan for the next steps."

"Right, it's not over. She has options," I said to him before hanging up.

At the next light, I called Emily. No answer. My heart sank. Why couldn't I find her?

The GPS said it would take 53 minutes to get home. When I plugged Emily's address in, it said 14 minutes. I'd never made a house call to a student, but neither had I encountered a situation like this: a terminated student who vanished.

She'd told me she didn't own a car. She wanted to lead the urban life in D.C. and save on that expense. But we weren't an urban campus, a mile away from the metro station. Today she could've taken the metro, a bus, an Uber. Or someone gave her a ride.

I followed the terse, efficient commands of the GPS to a narrow street, obviously constructed before rows of parked cars on either side left only a single lane in the middle. I had to hang back to let the car coming the other way pass. Yes, it took fourteen minutes to get there, but twenty-five minutes to find a spot. Luckily, I had the sedan rather than the minivan.

When I first moved to the D.C. area, I was surprised to learn that beautiful Victorians lined many of the streets. Emily lived in one off U Street that was obviously a rental property in need of renovation. I expected the front door, made of wood and glass, to be locked. An array of buttons signified the various apartment units by letter. I buzzed her apartment.

The temperature had dropped as the light waned. I'd grabbed my purse but hadn't bothered with my fleece, still overheated from all the stressful conversations of the day. I twisted the knob, desperate to escape the cold, and was surprised when it turned in my hand. Following the letters on the units, I climbed to the third floor. The steps creaked and groaned under my weight, and the hardwoods were faded and scratched—typical for a student dwelling. Breathing hard after the three flights of stairs, I rapped on the door with my knuckles. I tried a few more times, then texted, voicing my concern and telling her I was outside her apartment. My breathing quieted, and I reached for the knob.

Just like at the front door, it turned in my hand. What did this mean? I pushed the door open a crack. "Emily?"

Complete silence—not even traffic on U Street. I shoved at the door, and a wave of toxic gas greeted me. I pulled the neck of my sweater over my nose and mouth and gave a muffled shout. "Emily!"

Her body lay next to a wooden coffee table. I rushed over, my purse dropping, and gasped. Her eyes stared blankly, gray, leeched of life.

"No, no, no, no," I moaned, raising my gaze away from the horror. In a detached portion of my mind, I recognized my response as denial.

In the small kitchen beyond, a blue ring of flame whooshed at high heat.

I staggered to my feet and rushed over. With my hand pressing the scratchy fabric of my sweater to my mouth, I twisted the burner off. Averting my eyes from Emily's body, I snatched up my purse, hurried out of the apartment and into the landing where the air hadn't become saturated with the vile smell. Items: earrings, paper clips, a bobby pin, a paper clasp—conspired to form chains around my phone, which I finally fished out. With trembling fingers, I dialed emergency. My voice sounded surprisingly strong as I recited my name, used the police lingo of a *welfare check* on one of my students—and what I'd found.

"Are you requesting medical at this time?" asked the dispatcher.

"It's too late for that. But there's a strong smell of gas in her apartment building. I don't know who else lives here, but—"

"We'll send the fire department." She gave me instructions: open windows to get a cross-breeze, exit the building, and avoid turning on lights. She implied that the whole building could explode, so I hurried to the big window that faced the street, the *what if*s starting: What if I hadn't encouraged Sergeant Bronson to talk? I could have gone after her then, saved her from this.

I couldn't have predicted this I couldn't have prevented it. Mentally, I pulled myself away from this unproductive line of thought as I twisted the lock, pulling up the dusty, splintering frame. They were easy to raise compared to our townhome's, which had to be turned, levered, and raised in sequence to open. It made me think how easy it would be to break in through a window. Though she was on the second floor, somebody could have come up from the first floor.

I leaned my head out the window to get a lungful of clean air and wondered if I had already taken in a poisonous amount of the gas. I felt disoriented, but that could've been more from the shock than from the physical effects of the poisoning.

The cold made my eyes water and my nose sting. The narrow street below was quiet. I wondered how the fire truck would fit, and at that moment, I heard the wail of a siren.

I ducked back into the room. The dining room displayed another large window, matching this one. The light wood of an Ikea-style kitchen table clashed with the dark floorboards. Stacked against the wall were books. A few I recognized from our program, and a jolt of sadness and loss hit me.

Dusting off my hands, I kept moving, the warmth of my breath against the fabric of my turtleneck covering my mouth and nose. In the bedroom was an unmade bed pushed against the wall. The drapes were closed as if she'd left in a hurry that morning. Did she know then what she was going to do? Or was it a more impulsive act?

I swallowed, queasy—whether the sight of her body, being faced with her death, or the evil smell of gas that permeated the apartment.

I flung open the drapes and pushed the window up. The sun appeared for the first time that day as it sunk below the skyline of surrounding buildings.

The siren screamed its way closer. I leaned out the window and gulped in frigid air. Emily was a strong student, used to getting high grades, and the failure of the placement was a blow to her self-esteem. If only she'd seen that losing the placement wasn't the worst thing in the world. We would've found her another one. I wished I'd had the opportunity to tell her that.

A ring startled me. I dashed out of the bedroom to find the noise emanating from the phone beside Emily. It must've been in her back pocket, or she'd held it as she fell.

I snatched up the phone. "Hello."

I sensed confusion in the silence over the line until a man's voice said, "Is this Emily?"

"Who's this?" I asked.

"Jack Randolph, I'm an officer with D.C. Metro Police. Why are you answering Emily Vinter's phone?"

"When did you last see her?" I asked. When he paused, I added, "I'm sorry, I'm one of Emily's professors. I came to check—"

He interrupted. "Is she all right?"

Now, it was my turn to pause, unsure what to tell him.

His voice rose in pitch with agitation. "Is she there? Let me talk to her."

"The police are coming," I said. "You'll have to talk to them." I wanted to say, *wait until the police say it's all right*, but he'd already hung up.

The neighbors! Emily's unit was on the third floor. I knocked on the door in the hallway opposite. "There's a gas leak in the building! Everyone must evacuate!" Galloping down the next two floors, I shouted the same message, pounding on each door.

Hurrying out the front, I ensured the door remained open to allow emergency access. I was surprised no one in the building had followed. There weren't many units, so perhaps everyone was at work, safe from the horror here.

As the enormous fire truck rounded the corner, the siren's deafening wail blared out of time to its red flashers. Covering one ear, I held my phone to the other and dialed my husband.

"Where have you been?" Seth asked. "All the kids say is, 'Where's Mom? I want Mom.'"

And I wanted nothing more than to see them and hug them close—innocent and full of life. Tears jumped into my eyes.

As if he could sense them, my husband said, "What's going on? Are you all right?"

I reassured Seth that I was safe, just shaken and shocked. I gave an abbreviated version of events, ending with, "The firefighters just pulled up."

"Do you know when you'll be back?" he asked.

As I answered, I shoved my finger deeper into my other ear to block out the siren. "A couple of hours, I would think. You might need to feed them and put them to bed."

He said all the right things, reassuring me that everything would be fine on the homestead. It was exactly what I needed to hear.

Even though they were used to dealing with emergencies, the firefighters seemed to take an inordinate amount of time to wedge the truck in the street and park it. They were too late to save Emily, but the building might blow at any moment. Warily, I glanced at it again and moved further down the street.

Male voices called to each other, and the brake released with a heavy hiss. A blond and mustachioed fireman, towering in his boots, cap, and gear, spotted me on the sidewalk but trudged to the back of the truck without acknowledgment.

"Hello, I was the one who called," I said.

He eyed me warily as I approached. They must be so used to crazy and hysterical people approaching. In as calm a voice as I could muster, I explained about the state of her body, the burner, and the windows I'd opened.

"Okay, wait out here. Stay back," he said, tersely. The pulse of the emergency light lit up one side of his face an eerie blue, then the other red.

Just then, two police cars screeched around the corner and jerked to a stop, their sirens falling mercifully silent. Out of one emerged a heavyweight young white woman with a cabbage-patch face and a French braid bun; the other vehicle disgorged a lanky man with a potbelly—too old for patrol with the deep pockmarks that slanted down his face.

I waited for the arrival of Officer Jack Randolph. The street was now filled with emergency vehicles, blocking cars from entering or exiting. Fifteen minutes had passed since his call. It seemed like much longer. I wondered if I'd recognize him since I'd only caught a glimpse of him in the driver's seat yesterday when he'd dropped off Emily.

At that, a white Ford truck squealed around the corner and lurched to a stop at the perimeter of the emergency crew. A man jumped out.

He was shorter than I'd imagined. The picture I'd conjured of the dashing man who had swept Emily off her feet fulfilled the usual tall, dark, handsome stereotype.

I started to head him off—no one should see a partner like that—but he started jogging and slipped into the building entrance. I would catch him on the way back out when he might be more amenable to processing what had just happened.

As I waited, I called Adam, and he picked up right away. When I told him our worst fears were realized, he gasped, "Oh, my God. And you had to find her—terrible."

My throat knotted with tears at sympathy, and I cleared my voice to speak. "I knew Emily was obsessed with this young woman she'd met on a call, and she mentioned having insomnia. Her relationships with the other students were strained and the police department was an unpopular placement right now."

"Was this one of those copycat cases?" he asked.

Taken aback, I asked, "At the graduate school level?"

"Many of the students are pretty immature." Adam made a nice understatement.

"Emily thought being 'fired'"—I gave my voice the inflection of air quotes— "was the worst thing in the world."

"You can't get fired from a field placement!" The outrage in his voice rang through the phone.

My breath hovered visibly in the frigid air. "She wasn't thinking rationally."

Despite my words, I returned to my litany of *maybe*s and *what ifs*. *Maybe* I should have taken Emily's interference in police business more seriously and told her in no uncertain terms to stop. On the other hand, we taught our students, especially when they were in "host" settings, like police departments, schools, and hospitals, to question and to think about organizations critically.

"Ending a field placement is not the end of the world," Adam said. "Absolute worst-case scenario, she has a summer placement." I huddled against the chill, agreeing with Adam, until he said, "I'm going to have to let the dean know."

Avoiding a strong gust of wind, I tried to burrow, turtle-like, into my sweater. Of course, it would have to be done, but I was afraid it would add another reason to close down the program. A suicide—so much liability. Dean Bingham might find a way to blame me—the field placement was one I had started and was responsible for. He'd claim I put too much pressure on her to make the study succeed.

The fire engine churned and rumbled, and the smell of exhaust permeated the air. I didn't hear Jack Randolph jogging back down until his shadowy form emerged from the outer door.

"I was the one who answered Emily's phone. I'm sorry I couldn't tell you more." I studied him. In the streetlight, no tears shone in his eyes. Everyone's grief differed, so I couldn't judge him for that. "I didn't want you to see—" I broke off.

He'd covered the ground from the building to the sidewalk in a few quick steps, almost as if he was running away. Of course, I couldn't blame him, but neither could I let him go.

I hustled to close the distance between us. "Are you okay? This must be so hard."

He waved an arm in dismissal, and a frown bisected his brow. My empathy must have hit home. "I didn't know how sick Emily was."

His answer was unexpected, but I recovered. "Neither did we," I said, wanting him to see us on the same side before I launched into fact-finding. "Do you know why Emily went to Sergeant Bronson?" I had a hard time forming the words around what felt like my frozen lips. Plus, I was confronting a possibly dangerous police officer who might have had something to do with Emily's death. I swallowed and went on. "Emily had a theory about the suicide last Sunday night."

"Yeah, yeah, Emily thought it was murder."

"Why?" I said as if that was the most baffling thing I'd ever heard.

He shifted his eyes toward the fire truck, the blue lights reflecting in what had been the dark pits of his eyes. A stiff jaw and old acne scars gave him an aggressive edge. "She worked with the girl before, felt guilty, I guess, that she couldn't save her."

I reached out a hand in the air. "But we can't be responsible—"

The brown leather of his jacket squeaked as he raised his shoulders helplessly. "The self-inflicted gunshot—it gave her ideas."

I winced at the term but realized he was discussing the contagion effect like Adam and I had.

"Emily over-identified with the victim." He gazed at the flashing lights as if mesmerized.

I was surprised at his level of insight, then realized that Emily must have told him that herself.

While I worked that out, he shifted restlessly, and the dark hid his face again. "I told Emily to stop, but she even found the same doctors as that girl and started seeing them. Sick, right?"

Desperation gripped me as Jack started to leave. "And there's no way, right, from your reading of that scene Sunday night, that it could've been murder?"

"Naw." He balled his fists into the pockets of his coat. "A note and a self-inflicted gunshot to the chest." He shook his head, and I wondered about the slight smile on his lips. Rueful or something more sinister. "Not the easiest way to go."

I forced myself to keep following despite his air of danger. This was my only chance to talk to him before he jumped in his truck and roared off. I spewed some remaining facts: "Emily mentioned about the wrong hand, and the girl was anti-gun."

I knew the remark might be inflammatory to someone who carried a gun, but he didn't stop. Over his shoulder, he tossed, "The obvious answer is usually the right one."

"When did you last see her?" I asked as he picked up the pace. I followed.

"Two days ago," he called back to me without turning around. "I was trying to cool it. I could see she had too many problems."

"Do you have someone to call?" I shouted after him to be heard over the fire engines. "It's not good to be alone right now."

"Yeah, I'm fine."

Was he back with the girlfriend he'd probably never left?

After Jack had reversed and swerved off, I set out in search of my sedan amidst the ongoing commotion of fire trucks and patrol cars. A tremor shook me inside after our conversation. Jack was trying to downplay his involvement with Emily. Then why had he called and raced over here? Was he setting up an alibi that he couldn't have been involved in her death?

Inside the car, I reached for my fleece and shrugged into it as I started the engine to create a cocoon of warmth within the vehicle. I placed my hands near the air vents, hoping to dispel the cold that had settled in my bones.

As I glanced into the rear-view mirror, I noticed a police car with its unmistakable oblong headlights approaching. Judging from the timing, it could only be the patrol supervisor or the assigned detective. I hoped that it wasn't Sergeant Bronson they had sent. Would he even feel remorse for his role in Emily's termination and the subsequent chain of events?

The driver of the police car leisurely emerged and strolled toward Emily's building. I fumbled for my door handle and stepped out, eager to recount my side of the story to someone in charge.

As the figure approached, I recognized the familiar shape of a heavyset woman, slightly shorter than myself. "Sergeant Reynolds?" I called out into the darkness.

"Who's that?" Her voice was querulous.

"Cara Knight." I walked toward the woman. "You're back from maternity leave?"

Moving into the light of a nearby streetlamp, Sergeant Reynolds' full-length parka added bulk to her figure. Her hairstyle had changed since I'd seen her, with a side part and a straight cut to the chin. "Just got back last week," she replied.

"How's your newborn?" I forced myself to ask. I had little interest in discussing babies but had to join with her somehow.

"Oh, she's a pistol." Warmth was evident in her voice despite her words.

Like me, she was getting on in years to be having children, though she already had two older ones. Not like me, who had to hurry up and get it done at once.

"How old are yours now?" she asked me.

I went through the obligatory small talk about kids, glad Sergeant Reynolds was warming up to me. No sooner had I thought that than her demeanor shifted, and her tone became sharp. "Now, what are you doing out here?"

"The victim." I started with police speak to ingratiate myself into her world. "Emily Vinter. She was a student of mine. She had a practicum at Victim Services."

"I heard." She stamped her boots against the sidewalk, either cold or impatient to get inside. "She had a run-in with Bronson."

Realizing that gossip had already spread among the homicide unit, I continued, "Because of him, she was terminated from her placement."

"Why do you keep turning up?" she asked, banging her fist against her leg in annoyance. "I suppose you already trod all over my crime scene, poking around for yourself. Miss Nosy."

"I was worried about Emily. She left the police department suddenly, leaving behind her laptop. My director and I decided that I should do a wellness check." I wanted to show I hadn't acted without reason or consult. "When I arrived, it was too late." My throat closed up, and I swallowed until words could return. "The dispatcher told me to open windows, and then her phone rang, so I did pick up."

"Oh, for—" she exclaimed, the disgust in her voice evident. She wasn't joking around anymore.

Anxious not to be shut out of her investigation, I explained, "I'd just gotten here, and it hadn't fully sunk in that I was at a crime scene. I jumped to the obvious conclusion that she had done this to herself. But now I'm not so sure," I clarified.

Sergeant Reynolds stared up at the building, which was silhouetted in darkness now, none of the open windows visible, as if bracing herself for what lay ahead. I seized the opportunity to share my suspicions about the unlocked doors and the potential premeditation behind the scene.

She made a face, clearly not yet having formulated any conclusions. "Maybe she wanted people to find her body without having trouble getting in."

Sensing her impatience, I jumped to the next point. "Apparently, she was dating a patrol officer, Jack Randolph. He was the one that called her phone."

Sergeant Reynolds started toward the building entrance, her attention slipping away. "Who?"

"Jack Randolph—you know the guy, patrol, Northwest?" I didn't know the police district name, so referred to the area of D.C.

"Yeah?" She ambled along to the brick that led up to the front door, now propped open by weighted blocks that the firefighters must have produced. "Did you tell him?" she threw behind her shoulder. "That his girlfriend was dead?"

Inwardly balking at her attempt to push me away with insensitive talk, I bravely continued. "Isn't he dating April Owen, another officer?"

She twirled a carefree hand in the air to indicate our conversation was over. I stopped on the narrow sidewalk, knowing to follow anymore would shut me out completely. I called out one last question before she entered the dark abyss of the doors.

"Why would Emily deny that Siobhan Weaver's was a suicide and then take her own life days later?"

Sergeant Reynolds turned, her figure now in shadow. "That's more your end. The psychology."

Chapter Six

Thursday Morning

I relished the sense of normalcy as I accompanied my kids into preschool that morning. Behind us was another mother who had crossed paths with me a couple of times before at the drop-off. She looked polished in thin-plaid business slacks, a stylish long winter coat, and an accessorized scarf. Her little boy, Dylan, wore jeans and seemed delicate and shy.

As my son, dressed in brown cords and an orange long-sleeved shirt, excitedly dashed into the Two's classroom, the woman asked, "Is that Noah?" She mentioned that her son talked about Noah often, and I couldn't help but feel a hint of pride. Noah was undoubtedly the rock star of the class now that he was without a bib and pacifier.

Trying to engage Dylan in conversation, I asked him, "Who's this?" but he nestled into his mother's leg, too timid to respond. Though Noah had never mentioned her son, I was accustomed to hearing such statements about my son's popularity. I asked about her work instead to avoid making a false statement about her child. I was probably supposed to say, *where do you work outside the home*? That phrasing was not only mechanical, but it was also awkward. No one would be dressed up like that only to go home and clean up breakfast dishes.

"American University." The woman had salt and pepper hair, cut stylishly short. "I'm in Public Health."

We moved down the hallway out of the way of the kids arriving with backpacks bigger than themselves. I didn't try to trade first names with her. I might remember her son's name but not hers. "Oh, I teach, too—at Virginia University."

She frowned in confusion. "You drive down to Richmond?"

I got that question a lot, so my answer was canned. "I work at an off-campus program up here that nobody knows about." I had delivered it jokingly, but she didn't smile. I hoped to connect with more mothers here beyond those congregating on the playground after dismissal. But I was somehow in between: closer to stay-at-home moms with a flexible schedule but also with more to balance, and, let's face it, my kids were harder. I barely ever saw this mother; her partner—or nanny—must have been typically involved in Dylan's transport.

As she moved off to take Dylan by the hand into the classroom, I didn't sense that I'd connected with her either. He was still hanging back. The other kids were running around the tables, boisterous on the verge of chaos.

The preschool teacher, Daphne, gave a loud warning. "Friends!"

It was time to leave Daphne to it. She didn't go by the *Morah*—teacher—title that the others did. Despite her informality, the kids listened to her, and they all wanted to sit on her lap.

I went to bid a last goodbye to Alyssa. Arriving at the Three's classroom, I was greeted by Alyssa, twirling in a frothy Disney-style ball gown, complete with plastic, sparkly heels.

Catching sight of me, she called, "Mama, how do I look?"

"Beautiful!" I applauded her elegance. I had tried for gender-neutral clothing when she was a baby. However, as soon as she was exposed to Disney dress-up, she embraced it with as much enthusiasm as I would have done as a child.

The teaching assistant, Morah Claudette, just out of college, said, "Alyssa does this every day—the same dress, the same heels."

"How cute!"

Morah Claudette nodded without smiling, seemingly weary of the routine. I kneeled in front of Alyssa like her prince, asking for her hand in marriage. I hugged her goodbye, breathing her in, feeling the scratchy lace sleeves of her ball gown. I was reluctant to leave my children in all their warmth and liveliness. At work, I would be thrust back into the death of my student.

* * *

After I finally made it in and showed up at Adam's door, he waved me in. Too bright from the overhead lighting, his office was large but his desk, pushed into the back corner, didn't take up much space. He had the usual wall of bookshelves and various plaques, the designs on the book spines provided the only color.

Adam was about twenty years older than me, and the sorrow of the situation pulled his face into lines. He gestured that I should take one of the chairs in front of the desk.

"I've already spoken to the dean," he murmured as if keeping his conversation with the dean in complete confidentiality. "He wants to keep this hushed, as discreet as possible."

"Like a cover-up?" I inquired.

He scurried behind his desk. Seeing me still standing, he frowned. "It's not a cover-up, just avoiding unnecessary attention. We can't risk tarnishing our reputation with rumors of unstable students or accusations we're somehow to blame. The dean is worried about how this might affect enrollment next year."

Sitting, I scoffed, unable to hold back my sarcasm. "Well, it's good to know he has his priorities straight."

Adam's eyes narrowed, irritated by my remark. "No emails."

"Why not?" I asked, puzzled. It had always been standard practice to share sad news through email. "What about the dean's so-called transparency?" It was one of his favorite buzzwords.

"He says that's her parents' wishes." He shook his head in sympathy at them.

"Those poor people," I mumbled, my mind recoiling at the unimaginable pain of losing a loved one in such a manner.

Our moment of shared empathy was shattered when he cleared his throat and broached a sensitive topic. "The dean asked why you went to her place."

"I was worried. I called you, remember? You gave me her address." My voice was injured.

Adam turned up his palm as if pleading for understanding. "I'm just telling you what he asked."

I couldn't tell Adam that the dean might exploit this tragedy to close the Northern Virginia program. Adam would be pushed into retirement. He might not be so passive if he knew Dean Bingham's plans. I wasn't feeling much loyalty to the dean, but he had explicitly told me to keep the possible closing quiet. Why had he put me in such a position?

"Um, the dean was also wondering why you didn't involve the police, let them handle it?"

"The police *were* involved. She had just left there." I leaned forward for emphasis. And the *police*," I enunciated, "had just dismissed her." I raised my finger. "In fact, the police department can be held culpable. They didn't have a proper learning plan, which counselors she would shadow to learn from, and which kinds of cases she could support. They pretty much ignored and isolated her, to the point of it being relational aggression."

His white eyebrows raised. I wasn't sure he had heard the term before.

"There was no due process on her firing," I continued. "They hadn't made use of our process. We didn't have any written plan of remediation, nothing."

As I ended my speech, Rochelle entered, her hand to her mouth. "My God, I just heard."

"She found the body," Adam said, almost accusingly, at me.

Rochelle moved to touch my arm. "Oh, that must have been so awful."

I nodded, swallowing back the emotion her sympathy evoked. Once I could speak again, I related what had happened.

"We had no idea she was so fragile," Rochelle murmured after I'd finished.

And I hadn't even told Rochelle what Emily's boyfriend had said about her.

"You didn't see any of this before?" Adam asked me. "You teach the clinical courses."

"A little anxious, yes. Some of the best students are. Introverted, shy?" I nodded. "Rochelle didn't see it either," I pointed out.

Rochelle shook her head. "A perfectionist—losing the placement, she must have felt like a total failure. Textbook."

Wasn't it a little too textbook? Emily had thought the same thing about Siobhan's suicide: it was all a bit pat. How could Emily have done the same thing after that?

* * *

The rest of the week produced nothing additional in the way of the case, although I managed to secure a meeting with Anita Ware, the director at Victim Services, and Kaitlyn, her right-hand person, for Monday. Given all that had happened, we needed a heart-to-heart. They deserved a lot of blame in my eyes. She was focused on doing the right thing by a victim she'd worked with. Maybe she had been misguided and had seen murder, perhaps not wanting to accept suicide, given her identification with the victim.

On Saturday, our family routine took us down to the National Mall with the double stroller. At the National History Museum, the kids were enthralled by the replica of a woolly mammoth in the domed entryway. Then they got giggly when I said, "He looks like a Snuffleupagus." I could always get them laughing by saying that character's name from Sesame Street.

When we left after a couple of hours, I commended Seth's expertise in folding the stroller back into its compact form. This skill eluded me, leading me to insert the entire thing, with the children safely removed, into the back of the minivan.

During our little venture, I discovered in the back seat Emily's backpack, which I'd retrieved from the police department. In a panic, I'd run upstairs to her apartment. Too late, the bag had lost relevance. Now, I would have to wait to get into it. I didn't want to do it around the kids.

Seth and I had devised a strategy for the weekend: taking turns with childcare, each of us having an hour on and an hour off. I spent time with Noah rolling cars on the hardwood floors and attended a pretend tea party with Alyssa, which Noah literally crashed. I captured pictures of them at cute moments, the backs of their innocent heads, as they stood next to each other doing an art project at the easel we kept in the dining room space. The pictures made it look like we had a wonderful weekend.

After a round of trade-offs, we eventually allowed a movie while Seth went upstairs to nap, exhausted from throwing a ball back and forth with Noah. It ended badly when Noah hurled the ball into Seth's glasses, showing only defiance rather than remorse.

I sat on the couch with the kids in front of the TV on the little Elmo sofa, eating Pirate's Booty. It seemed like a violation to look into Emily's backpack. But it didn't matter anymore to her, right? Emily's last words were that she'd found something interesting in the data.

Amid spiral notebooks was her laptop, which demanded a password when I opened it. I started with *Emily Vinter* in all its variations—capitals, small letters, various punctuations between the words, periods, underscore, and initials.

Nothing.

I tried her boyfriend's name, Jack, his last name, both names and so forth. I recognized that a laptop password was a long-term commitment and probably predated Jack Randolph.

Frustrated, I turned my attention to the rest of the backpack. When I hit the small, zippered pouch and encountered a stack of pantyliners, the natural impulse was to recoil. But I forced myself to search underneath them, turning up something hard.

Hello?!

I pulled out a capsule-looking thing—a tiny vial filled with white powder. It was a coke dispenser. The gadget looked much too complicated; I usually relied on Seth to open packaging and bottles.

Was Emily a coke user? Wow, hard to believe, but I shouldn't be surprised. I'd played therapist long enough to know that ordinary outward appearances often concealed secrets.

Now, what to do with it? I certainly didn't want her parents to discover the vial. I'd give it to Sergeant Reynolds along with the backpack. I'd leave her a message first thing to see if we could meet after I finished with Anita tomorrow.

Did the coke have anything to do with her death? Did she get too depressed coming down? For the first time, I seriously considered that maybe she had taken her own life.

Chapter Seven

**Week 2
Monday Morning**

The following day, Seth, the kids and I set off as a family affair to do preschool drop-off. Once the kids were ensconced inside, I assumed the driver role as Seth, donning headphones, got on a phone call, much jollier in tone than when we'd all been together as a family. I worked north on I-395, crossing the 14th Street Bridge to D.C. I could see why Seth complained about his daily journey.

The GPS finally delivered me to the central Metro D.C. police station, its bleached stone façade ornate compared to the practical styles of most government buildings. I was a block down before finding a spot to swerve into. Seth was still talking, so I sketched a wave goodbye.

Inside, the Victim Services receptionist glared at me as I walked in and asked for Anita and Kaitlyn. "Kaitlyn isn't here," she snapped.

I rebounded quickly. "How about Anita Ware? That's who I set up the meeting with." Anita had told me that Kaitlyn would attend.

Instead of replying to me, the receptionist barked, "Your meeting's here," through a microphone that I couldn't see. Then she busied herself studying the computer monitor and ignoring me.

I expected Anita's usual uniform of skinny jeans, high-heeled boots, and a blazer. With the attire, her widely spaced eyes, black hair, and a big smile, she looked more like a country and western singer than anything else. But when she emerged to the waiting area, Anita surprised me by wearing a designer sweatsuit and platform tennis shoes. "Thanks for coming in early," she said, reaching for a hug. "I'm so sorry," she said into my hair.

I could have done without the touchy-feely stuff. We might have to have some tough conversations about how they had mishandled the evidence.

When she released me, she said, "This is when I try to get my walk in before the day gets going. Is it okay if we do that?"

"Of course," I said, but wished she'd told me she had an agenda in advance. I'd worn the clunky boots that were nice under a long skirt and leggings but not made for "walk and talks." I also carried Emily's backpack. I'd decided to give it and the vial to Sergeant Reynolds, not the Victim Services gang.

After the bells on the door of Victim Services rang behind us and we headed across the lobby to the front doors, I said, "It's just so shocking."

She turned and gazed into my eyes. "Oh, I know."

A balding officer passed on his way in. "Miss Anita," he said.

She put on one of her high beam smiles as we passed him. "How ya' doing, Rod?" After that, she waved at the cop manning the front desk. His stern demeanor cracked open when he gave a welcoming grin. Everybody around here sure seemed to love her.

I accelerated to keep up with her pace, and we were soon out the front entrance and down the street. I wore a medium-weight fleecy affair that downgraded my outfit to casual, but it was the softest warm coat I owned, and I'd needed that comfort today.

"Why don't you run it down for me? What happened?" Anita asked.

Tears came to my eyes from the sharp breeze. Dust swirled in the air, and scraps of dry leaves blew around as I told her the story. At least, telling it repeatedly was good for preventing the onset of PTSD. At this point, I had told Seth, the police officer at the scene, Sergeant Reynolds, Rochelle, and Adam, and now Anita.

Anita and I bustled along, passing a different brand of people than I saw in the 'burbs. Here, there were young professionals in long coats rushing down the street. I was in awe of women who walked quickly in heels much higher than mine. I wondered what it would be like to have a typical job and go to an office every day. In many ways, I did better with structure, but how could I spend as much time with the kids as I did now?

I pulled myself away from thoughts of an alternate career path. "How's Kaitlyn doing?" I asked.

"Fine!" Then Anita must've realized that she'd responded a little too brightly. "I told her to take a couple of days off."

To recover from her intern dying, or to stay out of the way until things died down? After all, Kaitlyn shouldn't have succumbed so easily to Sergeant Bronson's pressure to remove Emily from her placement.

The intrusive smell of marijuana invaded the air as we waited at the light. *Ah*, the scent of D.C. since they had semi-legalized it. District residents could have up to an ounce, but not buy it unless it was from a medical dispensary.

"Did Kaitlyn tell you what happened that day?" I asked.

Anita was vague on the details, other than how Emily had angered Sergeant Bronson. "You kind of have to be intimidating like that in homicide. Otherwise, the suspects and witnesses don't take you seriously." When she turned to me, Anita's cheeks were flushed from the cold.

I wanted to ask if he felt bad about it, but that would have been impertinent. "What was his reaction to hearing of Emily's death?"

She pursed her lips like she disagreed with him. "He sees her suicide as more evidence that her judgment was impaired. You have to understand Sergeant Bronson. His thing is serial killers."

Serial killers didn't fascinate me the way they seemed to everyone else. They killed repeatedly to gratify themselves. It all seemed so impersonal.

"But most homicides aren't serial killers. So, he doesn't like ninety-nine percent of what he does?" Was that like saying I love my teaching job except for the teaching?

She looked out toward the traffic whizzing by. "He's mad he has so many cases from when Sergeant Reynolds was out on maternity leave."

He must have seen her as getting away with something while he was working his ass off. I hated to remind people that if we didn't allow working women to give birth to babies, we wouldn't have many children.

On the back of my ankle, I felt the burn of a blossoming blister, so I thought I'd better get down to how I was going to access the data, and the work Emily had done on it. I phrased it as delicately as possible.

In answer, Anita said, "Yeah, I think Emily was crunching the numbers." Like most executive directors, her skill set was not in research. *Crunching the numbers* was literally pressing a button or two on a statistical program.

"I thought she was figuring out the sampling frame," I said. To Anita's frown of confusion, I explained, "I know the police department can pull up the stats of how many family violence cases patrol respond to in a certain period, but, apparently, they can't sort by Victim Services involvement. That meant Emily had to cross-reference Victim Services' client logs. Once she sorted that out, we would have to randomly select non-Victim Services cases that would be equal in number to the ones you all worked on. That's how we can compare them along the lines we discussed."

"I still think it's the individual officer and their decision, not anything else," she said. "We've won over a lot of people through my years here, but there's still a long way to go."

If Anita believed that was the sole reason, no wonder she and Kaitlyn curried favor with Sergeant Bronson. "And that may be," I said, not adding that was the point of research, to test hypotheses such as this one. "As you know, we can't look at individual officers, but we can see the sector and shift to see if that makes a difference. There's also ethnicity, gender, age, type of assault, and things like that which can be considered."

I switched the backpack to my other shoulder as Anita marched on, hands unencumbered, fists pumping, saying, "I know Emily already did a lot of work on it. She was stalled for a while getting the data from IT, but something must have shaken loose."

"Great!" I kept an upbeat tone. "Do you know how I can access the data?"

"Gee, I'm going to have to get back to you on that one," Anita said. "Hey, are you ready to turn around?"

In the other direction, we faced clogged traffic. The median spouted trees with scraggly, bleached branches poking into a moody sky. I wondered if it was going to rain before we made it back.

"Oh, there's April Owen." Anita raised a hand in a wave.

"Who?" In the navy Ford Explorer shooting by, a blonde woman lifted an arm.

"You know, Jack Randolph's girlfriend. That was another reason we didn't want Emily dating him. Do you want to tangle with a woman who carries a gun?" Anita jabbed me in the side with her elbow.

"Do you think being caught up in drama led to Emily taking her own life?" It was so cold I could see my breath in the air as I spoke.

"I'm sure it was all above her head, but who knows?" She shrugged, her mouth pulling down.

"Do you know April well?"

"Not as well as her twin, May. They're both cops, but very different."

"April *and* May?" Somebody got cute with the names. I was glad their mother hadn't had triplets and named the third one *June*.

"They're not alike at all. April is blonde and glamorous. May is short, a little heavy, a pixie cut. She's one of our biggest fans and calls us all the time. There's a third sister involved with CPS, a drug addict. Her parents are raising her two kids." She turned to me, perhaps realizing she was sharing a lot of gossip. "May is very open about her family history. She's been to therapy and all that."

"Okay, good," I said blandly as my mind went haywire. What if April, in a jealous rage, had followed Emily to her apartment and left her to die with the burner on? *What if, what if?*

"You said that Emily should've known not to mess with a woman that carries a gun. I'm sure you were joking," I smiled as I said this. "But I'm just wondering about her capacity for violence. I mean, her boyfriend—"

"They have a house together," she added.

"Wow, what are you going to tell Emily's parents about this?"

She shook her head emphatically. "We've referred them to the sheriff's office for counseling. We don't get involved in dual relationships."

I studied her. Okay, I could buy the argument that they couldn't treat Emily's parents as clients since Emily had interned there, and another agency had to handle them that way. But Anita and Kaitlin could at least tell the Vinters what happened that last day. It seemed they'd chosen to avoid that in the guise of an ethical consideration.

Outside the police station, Anita thanked me for walking with her and said she'd get back to me about the research. "I'm going in for a minute," I said. "To see Sergeant Reynolds."

Anita stiffened. "Sergeant Reynolds calls us the least out of all the homicide detectives."

That's how she judged each person here, apparently—how buddy-buddy they were with Victim Services. Anita gave me a hug, our bulky winter coats in the way. "We'll be in touch," she said.

When I entered Homicide, a burly detective sat at the front desk, doing a hunt and peck on a computer keyboard. "Can I help you?" he asked in a monotone voice.

"Is Sergeant Reynolds here?" I asked.

"Tell them I'm not here!" I heard her voice rise above the sectional furniture. "Tell them to go away."

He grunted and returned to the computer, looking depressed at his laborious progress.

"Sergeant Reynolds," I called. "It's me—Cara Knight."

In the ensuing silence, I glanced at the detective at the front, but his attention was on his fingers.

Finally, she spoke. "I know who you are."

"I just wanted to touch base briefly to find out what happened last night."

"You know what happened." A chair creaked, and she sighed. "You were right in the middle of it." She strolled out of the sectional divide. "Just like last time."

When I saw the dark shadows etched around her eyes, I asked, "Baby been waking up in the middle of the night?"

"Every two hours, and do you think my husband, that son of a—" She stopped herself from swearing, bowing her head and shaking it. "He won't wake up. He says he doesn't even hear her." She raised her head, eyes glaring. "She's screaming like someone's taking her by the arms and legs and pulling her apart, and he can't hear that?"

"This is probably not helpful, but my husband was the same way."

She didn't smile, so I hurried on. "After I left the other night, did anything else come to light—marks, defensive wounds, signs she'd been drugged?"

Hands on hips, she said, "Suicides suck, plain and simple. I don't know what else to tell you. And I don't have time to take your statement—too many homicides. I'll use the one you made with the patrol officer."

"Aren't you going to talk to Officer Randolph?" My voice had a pleading quality.

"Why would I do that?" she asked.

"He was seeing her. Maybe getting involved with him contributed to her death."

"Maybe, but I'm not getting into that."

I swung the backpack off my shoulder. "This is Emily's."

Gone was any sliver of humor. "You took something from the crime scene?"

"No," I explained quickly. "It was at the police department. I thought she'd left it behind. Then, with everything, I forgot I had it. I thought you might need it for evidence, though."

She made a face. "Evidence? Girl, I'm done with that one. I got assigned six straight cases since I've been back."

Somewhat sheepishly, I admitted to searching the backpack.

Her eyebrows shot up.

"I have a research project that Emily was working on related to family violence," I explained. "She had all the data. I was trying to find it." As Sergeant Reynolds continued to stare at me, I felt obliged to say more. "We put a lot of time into that research project. Anyway, I didn't get anywhere with that but did find a vial of coke. I can show you what pocket—"

Sergeant Reynolds shifted her weight. "Why can't you do your own job and not try to do mine for me? Do I get up there in front of your students and talk to them about Freud?" She started to turn around as if heading back into her cubicle, then said, "If she was doing coke, it'll come up in the autopsy."

"Or maybe it didn't belong to her," I said.

"Okay, it was in her backpack, but for the sake of argument, who would it have belonged to?"

"Well, what about Officer Randolph?"

"No, ma'am, we're not going there. And, if anything, she was hiding it from him. You have no reason to accuse him, and if you think I'm questioning him—" She gripped the backpack. "You know, people don't feel so good when they're doing coke. I hear that the first time is the best and that they keep chasing that initial high, and it's never so good again."

"I've heard that, too," I admitted, and then, seeing that I wasn't going to get anything else out of her, I turned to leave. Sergeant Bronson was bustling through the door to Homicide. His hair was darker than I'd remembered, or maybe it just needed a wash.

The man at the front desk raised his arm in a greeting but not his head. His tortuous progress reminded me of when I took the GRE or my comprehensive exams.

Sergeant Bronson's eyes went to Sergeant Reynolds, skipping over me. "Edna," he said.

"Arnie," she said back. No hellos or other salutations, no joking around. *Civil* was the word that I landed on to describe their interchange.

"Hello, Sergeant Bronson," I said. "We met the other day. I'm Cara Knight."

He looked in my direction, his gaze growing frosty. "I know who you are. I guess you're here again about that student, hell of a thing to have happened."

I noticed a clump of dandruff in his side part. "What was your reaction when you heard about her death?"

"Reaction?" He frowned. "I thought she was out of her mind. And angry."

Freud's original theory about depression was that it was anger turned inward.

"She was trying to get us back," he added. "An 'I'll show you.'" He let out a disgusted hiss that turned into a *Shit*. He looked up abruptly. "Excuse my language."

Here we went again. "You're saying she did it to get back at *you*?"

"At all of us."

But he was the one who had demanded that she be terminated immediately and had been broadcasting his opinion throughout Victim Services with his bellowing voice. I pictured Emily, humiliated, trying to escape.

One thing Sergeant Reynolds and Bronson were united on was getting rid of me. They walked me out, and then each headed off in different directions.

In the hallway, I glanced at my phone to check the time. It wasn't worth going all the way home and then doubling back to pick up the kids, so I figured I'd stop at a coffee shop between here and there and fish out the student papers I kept in my tote for these occasions.

As I passed the women's restroom, Anita emerged, along with a blonde patrol officer with so much mascara her lashes looked like tarantula legs.

"Hello again," I said to Anita, whose smile was strained. She didn't introduce me to the woman whom I now suspected was April Owen, Jack Randolph's girlfriend. She was dressed in regulation nylon and a bullet-proof vest, making even that look sexy. Even minus the gun, I would not have messed with her in a million years.

"Ma'am, prof, whatever you're called." The blonde spoke to me around a wad of gum. "That girl should never have been let in here. She was a disaster from the word go."

Anita had no choice now but to introduce me. With a clenched smile, she said, "Hey, April, this is Professor Cara Knight from Virginia University."

"Can you say more about that?" I asked April.

"Hard to believe she was in graduate school. She thought she was smarter than everyone, trying to tell us how to do our jobs, but she didn't know what she was getting into."

I decided to be daring and push for more. "I'm sorry she got involved in your—" I paused, searching for a non-offensive term. "Situation."

"We're good. She was just a flirt coming in here, throwing herself at him. Some girls just fall for the uniform."

I felt defensive on Emily's part. Jack had chased *her*.

"Shit, she was just a little student," April continued. "We've been together this month, Valentine's Day, five years."

April was brittle. Either she was lying to me or lying to herself. I didn't know what to say in the face of such raw denial.

"She got what was coming to her for sure," she said, her pink lipsticked mouth working a piece of gum in a shade that clashed.

Anita and I watched April stalk off, moving with unconscious sway and swagger. I did Anita a favor by not commenting on April's behavior. If there were ever someone who screamed *suspect*, it would be

April. Talk about motive. But I had no authority here to find out where April was that day and if anyone had seen her with Emily. Sergeant Reynolds certainly would not appreciate my returning to her with this tidbit. I had outworn my welcome for that day.

I decided instead to capitalize on the awkwardness with Anita. "Hey, I have an idea. Since I'm here, what about if I talk to the IT person that Emily was dealing with? Then I can find out the last step he was involved with and what needs to happen next."

When she hesitated, I used a little reverse psychology. "Would you come with me? Then, you can learn more about what we're trying to do. That sampling stuff can get tricky, and I can answer any questions he has rather than going back and forth through you, saving everyone a lot of time."

"Sure," she said, wanting to get rid of me now. "I'll walk you to the elevator since I need to badge you to go up."

The bank of elevators was only a few yards from where we stood. As she waved her badge inside an empty elevator that arrived, she said, "Fourth floor. His name is Ethan Banks. Let me know if he needs me to okay you. Bye now," she said as the elevator doors closed.

On the fourth floor, it wasn't obvious where Ethan was tucked away, since half the floor was devoted to dispatchers, who sat in sectional desks with laminated sides so their voices didn't carry to each other. All were women, white and Black, wearing blue and white uniforms that I would mistake for EMS if I saw them outside of here. A white woman, who looked about ten years older than me, was being pushed in a wheelchair by a middle-aged man. I couldn't tell by his expressionless demeanor if he was a paid caregiver, a partner, or a relative. The woman smiled at me, so I asked where the IT person had his office. She pointed the way, and I eventually located Ethan within a row of sectional furniture in a cubicle with no door. He was young enough to have caught the wave of Ethans that now populated my children's classes. Noah had two Ethans that he played with at the preschool playground: Ethan G. and Ethan E.

Ethan Banks, the IT guy, wore glasses and wavy hair that he technically didn't have to comb. The length of his hair alone tagged him as a civilian rather than police. He hunched behind a two-monitor set-up. With effort, he dragged his eyes away from the computer screens, which were reflected in his glasses, to me standing at the entrance to his cubicle.

"Yes?" he said, peevish.

When I explained myself, he said, "I gave it to that girl yesterday. Why don't you ask her if she's your student?"

"I guess you haven't heard." I delivered the bad news.

"Whoa." He straightened and shoved his glasses up to the bridge of his nose. "I didn't see that coming. She seemed okay when I talked to her."

I agreed that it did seem out of the blue, and we both recited some trite phrases about *how you never know*. I then explained that I still needed the data. "So, can you walk me through what needs to be done so I can access the files? You can talk to Anita Ware if there are any questions."

"I have to merge the platforms and get the two systems to share a code."

He'd undoubtedly learned one thing from being at the police department: how to spend more time getting out of work than actually doing it. He glanced at his monitor and said, "I can't do it now. I have a meeting with one of the deputy chiefs in five minutes. How about if I call you?"

Why did I think I was getting shined on again as I handed over my business card? I could see how frustrating this was and what a downer for Emily. She did have some risk factors—being ignored and isolated as an intern; the worry about making the research happen; a relationship that would probably not work out, for a variety of reasons; and, at the end, getting dismissed from the internship. With all that, did she decide that suicide was the only way out?

Chapter Eight

Monday Evening

That night, I headed into my living room, where CNN blared *Breaking News*, carrying two cups of kava tea. Although we talked throughout the day, this was the time Seth and I usually caught up, and I did work that didn't take as much mental capacity, like returning emails and typing edits into manuscripts. Editing was what I did when other mothers worked on crafts. I set down the mugs, wafting steam, and filled in Seth about my trip to the police department. Then he had some news for me.

"My mom enrolled in a rice diet program. She's done this one before. In North Carolina."

"She's flying out of state for a quack diet? Those aren't safe, and she'll just put back on the weight she loses. How much will it cost?"

He shook his head at my barrage of questions. "Maybe you can call her."

Aside from the usual Botox and chin zaps, I could sometimes talk her down from facelifts and other expensive plastic surgery. Of course, it was her money, she could spend it any way she wanted to. But, before doing so, she needed to hear a voice of reason.

Seth didn't try anymore, not wanting to get all roiled up. Usually, I didn't call Barbara. I figured Seth's daily call would suffice for the household, and I was afraid of starting something. It was the same as with children—I would do something special, like McDonald's fries after school once, and then they would expect it each day after that. Not only that, but they would expect it in exponential ways. A small Blizzard shared between them became a medium, each with extra Oreos.

"I'll call her tomorrow," I promised.

* * *

The next day, after dropping off the kids, I arrived late at the Smoot Lumber industrial park that I called my place of employment. I walked into the space that was comparable to the multi-purpose room at the preschool. It made me think about how nothing was cuter than hearing a two- and three-year-old speak about *the multi-purpose room.*

Roberto had set up two vats of coffee at the back. At the front of the room was Jane Ogden, the director of the MSW program, and Beverly Johnson, Rochelle's counterpart, the internship director from Richmond. Dean Bingham had arranged that they would drive up and lead the discussion with the students. They were in a more objective position as they hadn't known Emily beyond a name in the system.

None of the staff and faculty up here had a problem with that. I certainly didn't want to lead a process session for my students when I had to teach them research in an hour or so. The change in roles would be dizzying for all involved.

I hitched my patent leather briefcase over my shoulder as I headed toward the coffee. If it weren't for my mother-in-law's generous gift-giving, I wouldn't have any nice things. As thin, watery coffee dribbled into a paper cup, Jane spoke about the reason for the gathering and mouthed some of the usual phrases: *difficult time, a lot of feelings*, and *we're here to listen.*

I stirred in non-dairy creamer that would not dissolve under the ministrations of a tiny stick. We'd agreed not to tell the students I'd found her body. Just like I didn't tell them that I lived on the edge of the asphalt where they parked their cars, we wouldn't share specific details about her suicide. At first, the students only had questions that Jane and the field director deflected.

I tiptoed to a seat at the back and slid into a metal chair. About half of the full-time students were in attendance. From the back of the room, they looked identical, with long, flat-ironed, straight hair streaming down the backs of their sweatshirts. The mood was somber, and, for once, they were off their phones, their attention at the front of the room.

I tried to sip the coffee, but the smell made my stomach turn over. The heat through the cup made it almost too hot to hold, but I was grateful for the warmth after the raw cold outside and the reason for this meeting.

Beverly did allow an "It's hard to process this," ostensibly directed toward Jane, who murmured her agreement. The therapeutic gambit succeeded, and a student began to talk.

When it came to speaking up, there were two factions. Like the student speaking now, the first didn't hesitate to raise a hand and give an opinion. It had annoyed me as a student myself when one classmate constantly spoke up, but as an instructor, I was grateful. The other faction involved the type of student who never spoke to the point where it seemed withholding. However, they did surprisingly well on papers and tests.

To student comments, Beverly was particularly good at meaningful and expressive *mm*s and nods. "Thank you for sharing," was all Jane said. Guilt was the theme, as it often was with suicide: *If only I'd known how bad she felt. I wish I had reached out to ask how she was doing.*

When people could no longer tolerate the guilt in the room, the conversation took another turn: *We had no way of knowing. It wasn't our fault—she must have had a lot going on. We have a lot going on, too. If someone's determined to kill themselves, they will.*

I winced at the last one. I heard it every time I covered suicide assessment and always suggested gently that, given the survival extinct, people generally wanted to be pulled out of the way they felt by a supportive listener.

Among the young women in attendance was Lissa, whom I'd taught in foundation practice and now in research. She was barely five feet tall with a half-shaved head with the other half to her shoulders. She was outspoken, advocating for queer rights, among other things. Today, she was quiet and unusually fidgety. Her legs bounced up and down, and her arms were crossed against her chest. When the event ended, she grabbed her backpack and shot out the door. I gathered up my things and followed.

She was heading toward the restrooms in the main lobby so that it could have just been an emergency bathroom break, but I suspected more. "Lissa!" I called out. Our job in this situation was to help the students. Wasn't I helping?

She turned and stopped. "Oh, hi, Dr. Knight." Her voice was flat.

I caught up with her. "Are you all right?"

On cue, her eyes reddened.

Before she could say, *I'm fine*, which she obviously wasn't, I said, "Hey, let's take a break outside."

She didn't say anything, only nodded, and we walked in silence to the front doors.

Outside, I pointed to the right toward Smoot Lumber. "I know you had some classes with Emily, right?"

She nodded, studying the sidewalk as we strolled. "Yeah, it's a shock. But those people in there—" She shook her head, obviously choked up. Tears spilled over onto her cheeks. "Some of them were mean." She wiped at it. "I wasn't a good friend, either."

We had reached the Social Security Office. I never went over this far, although I directed many people lost in our wing searching for it. "What do you mean?" This was another stock-in-trade phrase for the helping professions and for being a college professor. I probably said this as often as I said "no" to my kids.

"I don't want to be a snitch," she said.

"Don't worry, this is confidential," I rushed to say rather than, *you're training to be a social worker, not a gang member.*

She sniffed. "Do you have a tissue?"

Did I have a tissue? I was carrying a briefcase slash diaper bag, for goodness' sake. Of course, I had a tissue. And diapers, granola bar, and a pack of wipes.

She dabbed at her eyes and said, "We had this group project in clinical practice. And we had big groups, like five apiece."

Even with fewer than four, the laggard syndrome abounded in group projects. Sure, I knew why instructors used them. They reduced grading by two-thirds, you could use class time for "group work," and the students' droning presentations didn't take so long in class.

"I was in Emily's group." She met my eye for the first time. "You know, she was really smart. So, me, Maddy, Holly, and Judy got with her."

Cliques were everywhere, unfortunately. They didn't end in middle school but continued into graduate school and beyond.

"Emily did most of the work." She raised her head again. "And in full disclosure, I have to be honest." She held her tissue to her face to hide the wobbling chin. "My partner left me at that time, and I just wasn't in a good headspace. I couldn't focus on classwork."

I clucked sympathetically but didn't want to interrupt the flow of her words. A truck bed clattered as it jounced over one of the speed bumps at the outer edge of the lot.

"Emily went to Dr. Barber-Rufus, telling her she had done almost all the work. Dr. Barber-Rufus called us in, but . . ." Lissa shrugged. "It was four against one. We said we had done our share, and that Emily was being unfair." She looked down. "Basically, we said she was OCD—she was a little. She had to have it perfect. And the other women—they didn't like being corrected all the time. And when we gave her anything, she would totally re-write it."

Social workers are an intuitive lot, so she sensed my unspoken question: *Why?*

"I told you, my headspace, plus you know I'm against the school having field placements at police departments and child welfare. I thought she should've advocated for change if she was going to be with the cops."

I thanked her for being so honest, though I was perturbed about her group's treatment of Emily. Emily hadn't shared it with me, but our interactions centered more on the research.

Lissa nodded solemnly. "I know we didn't make her kill herself, but . . ." Social isolation did a number on people's heads; we all knew that. She stared across the parking lot. "Hey, I'm going to get some coffee before I head to class, clear my head." That would make her late for her one o'clock, but it wasn't my class she was missing.

I wanted to go straight in and question Yvette, Dr. Barber-Rufus to the students, but when I returned to my office, I could hear her across the hallway shouting on the phone to her only child, fourteen-year-old Coco. It was even rumored that she picked up the phone for Coco in the classroom. And *I* was the one who got dinged for *my* teaching?

After talking with Lissa this morning, I started wondering whether Emily *had* killed herself. She was isolated socially among the students; she was romantically in what I could only assume was a complicated situation, and then she was abruptly terminated from her placement.

Maybe my suspicions about it possibly being murder were off, and I just didn't want to accept that a bright, attractive woman had done this to herself.

* * *

The next day, after our post-school playground time, the kids were watching *The Nightmare Before Christmas*. Alyssa feared *E.T.*, that adorable tyke, but the loose plot of a subversive Christmas was easy to follow. Alyssa and Noah munched on Pirate's Booty, sitting in their Elmo couch beside each other, looking adorable. There was nothing Alyssa and Noah would both eat except for that magical product, Pirate's Booty. Reminiscent of Cheetos but less ghastly in its color and artificiality, it had to be rationed because, like rats with cocaine, the kids couldn't stop on their own.

While they were occupied, I seized on the opportunity to call my mother-in-law, Barbara, and clean up the kitchen.

"Hello?" she moaned like a self-pitying walrus when she picked up. "Hi, Cara, I didn't even recognize your voice. I hadn't heard from you in so long."

The guilt-mongering was unnecessary, and I forged on, telling her about a time when Alyssa had mentioned Grammy recently. Our only commonality was the children, so I worked the angle.

"Aww, the little darling. Is she there now? Can I talk to her?"

I walked up the stairs. "Alyssa, do you want to talk to Grammy?"

Alyssa shook her head without changing her gaze from the screen.

"She's watching *The Nightmare Before Christmas* again." Young children weren't into the concept of talking on the phone. They were concrete and needed to have the person in front of them.

Barbara cackled. "Why does she like that so much?"

"The songs, the creatures?" I grabbed a sponge and ran it over the counter, catching crumbs in the palm of my other hand.

"It's so funny you let her watch that."

Ha ha. I turned the sponge on its bristly side to scrub at what seemed like a glue spill but was probably just hardened milk.

"I miss her so much," said Barbara.

"Then come back and see her." I wanted the kids to have people who loved them, even if this meant putting up with Barbara.

"I can't. I'm going to North Carolina. Basically, you eat rice. You can lose up to twenty pounds while you're there."

I ran the sponge under the faucet. "Seth mentioned that."

"I bet he did. He tells you everything."

I paused in surprise. Wasn't that marriage? "Why don't you just come here instead?" I asked again. I mean, what was she looking for in weight loss—love?

I had learned to wait out Barbara's silence and not hurry her. It triggered her when I repeated my question, thinking she hadn't heard me. *I'm thinking*, she'd say, testy.

This time, she said, "I can't. I'm going into this program next Friday."

I wasn't about to lecture her on sensible diet and exercise, so I said in a singsong voice, "I have a new mystery."

"How are you going to solve it if I'm not there?" she asked, alluding to the mystery we'd cracked the year before.

"That's what I'm saying." I took another run at the counter with the sponge.

The phone beeped that another call was coming through—Adam.

"Hey, Barbara, I'm sorry, my boss is calling." He wasn't my boss technically, since that was Dean Bingham, but I needed to convey generally that an authority figure was summoning me. "I need to take this."

By the time I got her to understand, Adam was gone. When I called back, he said, "Can you get over here? Emily's parents are on their way."

I said to Adam, "Now? I have the kids."

"Can't someone watch them?"

"Oof." I blew out air.

"Isn't there anyone you can call? Seth?"

"Seth isn't due until—" I craned my neck to see the digital time on the DVD player, that ancient device. "Four hours and fourteen minutes, but who's counting?"

"Please, I need you here, too, to talk to them. You're clinical."

I relented. "Let me see what I can do."

I was delighted when Rosa accepted the impromptu gig. Over the phone, she said, "I do that for you. You drive?"

"The kids just came home from preschool. They won't want to leave again. Can you walk?" It would probably take her fifteen minutes.

"You come pick up?" She was such an amiable person, but walking the few blocks to our townhome was where she dug in her heels, figuratively and literally.

When I relented, knowing I would not get the babysitting I needed unless I did, she said, "Leave in ten minutes."

I started the countdown as soon as I got off the phone. "Guys," I said, "We're leaving in ten minutes to get Rosa, okay?" You cannot make sudden movements with children. You must prepare them for the next move; otherwise, they become unglued.

They ignored me, entranced with a close-up of Sally and her stitched-up face. I had worked with a teenager once who had cut her face up like that by running through a French door on a runaway adventure.

At the appointed time, both Alyssa and Noah started wailing in protest. I tried to bribe them, keeping my voice upbeat like *we're all having fun here*. "You can finish the Pirate's Booty on the way! You can take it with you in the car!"

They weren't having any of it, and, as predicted, when I pulled into the loop of Rosa's condo building, both kids were crying in symphony. I raised my voice into my cellphone to be heard above the din. "We're here."

Faintly, I heard, "I come now."

When I leaned back against the headrest in defeat, I could watch the elevator lights and the numbers to descend. I was like a child or a dog, so eager for Rosa to appear.

Rosa had a big grin as she left her lobby and headed toward the minivan. We could only look on in misery. She turned to Noah as she entered the passenger side, "Why you crying?" She started a little ditty to distract him and performed dance moves in the front seat. "We be home. *Vamanos!*" She started clapping. She was just making more noise; none of her jolliness made them cry less.

My cell phone rang to add to the chaos. It was Adam. "Where are you?"

"Okay, I've got the babysitter," I said.

"I can't hear you," he shouted.

"I'll be there soon," I said, pulling out.

In our garage, as soon as I released him from the harness, sweating and red-faced, Noah sprang into my arms. I held him close. He thrust his hand down my blouse, trying to find the nipple he regressed to as his personal worry bead.

Rosa had seen it all, so I didn't remove his hand. I just wanted Noah to calm down before I had to rip myself away again to leave. She leered at his behavior. "Look at that! Oh, my goodness!"

He started what Seth and I called *open-mouthed crying* when I tried to slither off. No graceful way to do it; I finally had to pull away from his grasp, and Rosa had to hold him in place as he struggled in her arms. As she did, she tried to pretend they were dancing, and she broke into a happy melody. "Let's dance! Let's shake your body!"

Perhaps this gambit worked once I'd closed the door behind me. But I could hear his wails from outside.

The phone rang again. Seeing it was Adam, I set off briskly for the drainage ditch. "They're here," he said when I answered.

Chapter Nine

Wednesday Afternoon

Outside the building, I could see through the double glass doors that Adam was waiting for me in the lobby, looking out as eagerly as I had done minutes ago for Rosa. He held the door for me and immediately began talking.

"Emily's parents are in the restroom. They just drove all the way from Michigan." Depending on where they lived, it was at least a five-hour drive. "I've talked about it with the dean. He doesn't want you telling them it was you who found her body. He wants it to be the police, not us. And they should be the ones to tell them what happened, that losing the placement seemed to trigger her into—" He broke off and shook his head. "You tried to dissuade them from dropping her? It was an abrupt termination, and she took it badly. It's on them. We did everything we were supposed to. You made multiple visits to that placement."

The dean wanted Emily's parents to hold the police department liable, not our school.

"Isn't that going to come out at some point, that I found her?" I asked. "Then they'll wonder why I kept that back."

"Let's just cross that bridge when we—" He broke off as the Vinters emerged from their respective bathrooms.

My heart ached for Emily's parents. Gray was my primary impression: their fleece vests, pallor, hair, eyeglass frames. Mrs. Vinter's cargo pants were baggy as if she'd dropped a few pounds after hearing the awful news. Mr. Vinter's shoulders were stooped with grief.

Adam shook his head at me in sorrow before the couple came up, and we performed simultaneous introductions and condolences.

Emily's mother asked Adam, "You're the dean?"

Anyone would assume that of a tall, silver-haired white man. Adam explained that he administered our off-campus program.

I said, "Your daughter was in my research class—best student there."

"She was so smart. That's what I don't understand." Mrs. Vinter bowed her head and fumbled in her vest pocket for a tissue.

"It has nothing to do with that," I murmured, feeling that sense of helplessness that social workers navigate daily.

As Adam ushered them down the hallway to our office suite, Mrs. Vinter said, "We don't believe for a minute that she—" Mrs. Vinter had to swallow down the emotion before continuing. "But you've got to admit this place is pretty depressing. Hundreds of miles away from the main campus . . ."

"Two hundred," I admitted, for no good reason but to engage with them while gesturing that they should proceed through the door to the suite.

"I don't know if she'd have enrolled here if she knew she was so far away, and the work—so depressing," she said. "The homeless, drug addicts, women who their partners stabbed."

Once I actually worked with said people, I saw their humanity. Hearing their backstories, I realized there was no mystery as to why they'd ended up in their current straits—all judgment was gone.

"Did Emily say she found it depressing?" I asked as we streamed past Roberto at his desk at the entrance to the administrative offices. He knew the parents' names; he and Adam went to lunch daily. Roberto's face was so mournful he didn't look like himself.

"Let's go to my office, where we can sit down," Adam said, leading the way.

Mrs. Vinter answered, "She liked the work, helping. But she was frustrated at that police station. They hardly let her do anything."

Mr. Vinter shook his head. "She wasn't depressed."

"Was she ever?" I asked.

"You know how moody teens get," said her mother. "I guess she went through a phase like that."

"Finally, we just told her . . ." Mr. Vinter grimaced. "Look on the bright side, how much you have to be grateful for."

Probably one of the worst things you can say to a depressed person. I said, "Did she get help then, talk to anyone?"

"What could therapists tell her that we couldn't?" the mother said. "After all, no one can make anyone change. You have to make up your own mind."

There was admittedly a nugget of truth to her argument, although a therapist could undoubtedly facilitate the process. This was not the time to catalog the benefits of therapy, however.

"It was a bad idea," said Mrs. Vinter. "For her to come here on her own."

I couldn't see Mr. Vinter's eyes behind his frames when he said, "We wanted her to get into something with more of a future, not going into debt for a degree where she couldn't make the payments."

I guessed him for an engineer. Neither was this the time to argue the benefits of a graduate program in social work.

Mrs. Vinter shrugged. "Social work and psychology were the only things that interested her."

"It's natural for us to look back and think of the *what ifs*," I said.

"I do think about that—all the time," Mrs. Vinter said. "If she'd never chosen this degree. If she never chose *this* program. Why come all the way up here when there was another social work program closer to us?"

We were ranked higher in the *USA Today* rankings, another fact irrelevant for today's meeting.

"When did you last talk?" I pitched my voice low and calm.

"A week ago, Sunday." Mrs. Vinter looked to her husband for reassurance.

He nodded. "This Sunday, we didn't get a hold of her. That was the day she—" He broke off.

Mr. Vinter raised narrow shoulders. "We didn't think anything of it. She was busy. It was her last semester. And she was looking forward to graduating."

"Getting out of here." Mrs. Vinter said, looking around the sparse walls of Adam's office.

"One thing that we found strange . . ." Mr. Vinter turned to his wife rather than me to speak as if to get reassurance. "Emily said she might want to stay in D.C. after graduation. She'd always talked about leaving as soon as she finished school. This area wasn't what she expected."

I bet. What with the campus located a mile from the nearest metro station, Van Dorn, and D.C. being the "loneliest" city in the U.S., according to a national survey, I could see why she originally wanted to leave. Perhaps hooking up with Jack Randolph gave her a change of heart. But that would lead nowhere except straight back to the partner with whom he supposedly shared a house.

"Did your daughter have a boyfriend or a close friend she confided in?"

I saw Adam flash me a look, but I ignored him. Isn't this a question that people asked?

The couple read each other's expressions. The mother spoke first. "We moved around so much when Emily was in school."

He said, "I worked for a defense contractor. We followed the military around."

"It was hard for her to make friends when we were always leaving someplace," Mrs. Vinter resumed the train of talk.

There was research on the increased risk for suicidality with frequent moves in childhood. They did a number on one's head. However, I wasn't about to share that fact, so I switched topics.

"She was working on a research project for me," I said. "Did she mention that?"

"Yeah," Emily's dad said. "She was jazzed about it initially, but it didn't seem like it was working out."

"At least she could work alone," Mrs. Vinter added.

I waited for her to say more.

"Well, I mean that Emily always got used in those group projects." She clucked. "The good students carried the load for the lazy ones. Finally, she went to the professor. Dr. Barber-Rufus." She emphasized the name. I gave her full credit for getting it right. "Who did nothing. They all got A's, but it was all on Emily." She murmured, "If something were going to happen, I would have thought it was then."

Her husband's head snapped up.

"Was she seeing a therapist, do you know?" I asked.

They both stared at me, surprised. Then Mrs. Vinter turned to her husband. "Was she using our insurance for anything like that?"

He shrugged and let his shoulder drop in a defeated gesture. "I can check."

I couldn't imagine anyone checking their insurance records regularly. I would rather change a million of my own children's diapers than deal with insurance.

I held up a hand, volunteering. "Only if it's helpful, if you find out their names, I can speak to them for you, tell them what's happened, how to get a hold of you."

Stunned, the Vinters nodded, and I backed off and changed the subject. "Have you heard from the police?"

"After the initial call—" Mrs. Vinter stopped and swallowed as if sustaining a punch to the gut. "Nothing."

"We don't even know who he is," said the dad.

"Sergeant Edna Reynolds. I can give you her phone number." I shuffled around in my tote to spare him the embarrassment of recovering from the gender gaffe. Instead of a pen and my wallet with Sergeant Reynolds's business card, I turned up the honey oat bar I carried around for so long that the sealed package had given way. I pulled out my wallet. A paper clip hung onto the zipper, and oats dangled off that. I quickly detached the jetsam and rifled through my cards to find Sergeant Reynolds's and take a picture of it for them. By sending it to them, I would have their number, too.

* * *

At my desk, I marveled how little time had passed since I'd picked up Rosa. Now that I had asked her to babysit, I needed to make it worthwhile, at least a couple of hours more. I stood, unable to settle to work after the emotional intensity of the Vinters' grief. I crossed the hall to Yvette's office.

"Knock, knock," I said to Yvette, whose desk faced the side wall, meaning that her back was to the door. I startled too easily for a layout like that. I needed to see who was coming.

She beckoned me in, giving one of her big smiles that had helped her get to where she was. About ten years older than me and a foot taller, she scraped her curly hair into a bun and didn't mess with makeup.

She swiveled her chair to face me and slipped her feet out of a pair of stretched flats resembling slippers. "I hope you don't mind."

I gave a tense smile as foot odor wafted out from the flats. "Get comfortable. It's your office."

Gunter, an adorable Airedale, lay on his side, too knocked out to even say *hi*. Usually he showed up at my desk, grinning. He also served as a therapy dog for tax purposes. Perhaps that explained his fatigue. His nails were painted red.

Yvette saw me smiling at him. "Coco gave him a manicure."

"Cute." I sat in a blue and silver chair that was identical to my office's. Her office was made smaller than mine by more shelves and books and many more piles. A giant standing fan took center stage.

"I need pet therapy," I said, telling her about Adam's and my visit with Emily Vinter's parents as I stroked Gunter's soft fur. "Did Emily ever disclose in your class about depression anxiety? In clinical practice, they sometimes do." For a particular style of instructor, it was a way out, to turn the class into personal therapy or a bloody support group. Another way to get good evaluations—provide free therapy.

Yvette flapped her hands in front of her face, I thought to signal her distress at the tragedy of the Vinters, but she said, "I'm sorry, I have no estrogen left. Can you turn on the fan?"

I stretched out my arm to do her order—I was used to such commands from my mother-in-law—and my hair flew around like Medusa as I tilted it toward Yvette. "How's that?"

She smiled in approval, even though it was only recycled air from our windowless suite.

"Emily didn't say much in class. I call on them, though, if they're quiet."

Then why were *my* evaluations such crap? I would never put a student on the spot like that.

"I knew she was at Victim Services," Yvette went on. "Some people in the class were against a placement at the police department."

"We don't get into so much controversy in research class. The students are so anxious and resentful, they don't have the energy for causes."

Yvette nodded, turning toward her desk and snatching up a plastic wrap package containing an over-processed blueberry muffin. "Yeah, I didn't see any red flags."

"There was a group project that Emily worked on. I think it was in your class." I made my phrasing and tone questioning rather than accusing. "You know, where they present on a clinical topic and teach the class?"

Yvette wrestled with the packaging as she considered. The phone rang, and she frowned at it. "Sorry, I have to get this—it's Coco." She yelled into the phone, "Coco? What's wrong?" The muffin, still in its packaging, lay forgotten on her lap.

I bent down and petted Gunter, enjoying the feel of his curls through my fingers. He was roughly six times the size of Miffy, our dog.

"Well, call them back," Yvette continued in high volume. "Tell them we can do Friday. It's really not that hard, Coco." Coco fired back because Yvette straightened in her seat. "Excuse me, I teach tonight, and I've got to get some writing done before that. You have the day off."

Enmeshment, we called it in family therapy, when mother and child were interacting at the level of peers.

"Coco, they canceled Gunter's grooming appointment. You should have just made a new appointment then. Why not take care of it?"

Because you train her to call you for any little thing?

After a slight pause, Yvette said, "Okay, bye!" She clicked off her phone and fanned herself frantically. "That girl!"

"Emily Vinter?" I reminded her.

"I don't like them running to me like I'm Mommy to fix it. I told her to address it with her group. I would never deprive a student of that kind of learning opportunity."

I leaned forward. "After the debriefing session earlier, Lissa Panilla was crying. When I took her aside, she said she felt guilty."

Yvette's face didn't betray any reaction. She waited for me to finish.

"Lissa said when they met with you, the other women in the group lied about how much work they'd done, and Lissa went along with them."

"Huh," was all she said, and finally tore open the plastic with her teeth.

While she was so engaged, I took advantage. "Do you still have them do the process recording assignment?"

She nodded as she bit into the muffin.

"Do you have Emily's?"

She studied me, chewing thoughtfully. "Why?"

I had the grace to blush. "I'm working with her parents. They want to know more about her state of mind."

"Her assignments are probably on her computer." She batted off the crumbs that rested on her chest.

"We can't get into her computer because of passwords. Maybe you have them turn in a hard copy?"

"Yes, I can read them better that way."

"I know, I print some of mine, too." I graded the papers in different modalities, hoping for inspiration.

Yvette shoved another bite of blueberry muffin into her mouth. "FERPA?" Crumbs sprayed as she spoke.

Family Educational Rights and Privacy Act involved privacy protections in educational settings. When I was a student, I collected my papers from an envelope left outside the instructor's door. Such practices were now verboten.

Gunter leaped up from full-nap mode to alert and ready to take advantage. A dog beat a broom or vacuum to get those last crumbs off the ground. Even Miffy still did that.

"She wrote her first recording on a suicidal woman with maybe domestic violence?" She wrinkled her brow. "I returned that one to her immediately because I was waiting for it." Yvette eyed me. "You're getting too involved. There were signs that anyone could have caught. She wasn't bullied in my class. A couple of students opposed law enforcement or child welfare placements. I let them talk but wouldn't have let them attack Emily." She took another bite of her muffin and said through a full mouth, "You know, you couldn't have saved her either."

Therapists and their psychoanalyzing. Still, I flushed. "I know, but don't you think it's strange? Emily was looking into another woman's suicide, and then she supposedly dies by suicide?"

"Uh-uh. Emily shouldn't have been looking into anything. And neither should you. That's the police detectives' job, not yours." I could see how she exerted her authority in the classroom.

She bit down into the cake part of the muffin. Crumbs flew. Her phone rang again. "It's Coco again. I've got to get this."

I nodded and leaned over to pet Gunter who thumped her tail in appreciation as Yvette's voice rose. "Coco, you have to finish that paper for English before I get home. Then I told you I would read it. I can't do it for you." She swiveled in her chair to face her desk and rifled through papers as she listened. I lifted my head, as hopeful as Gunter at crumbs. The stacks gave me the impression that Yvette would never get around to finding, much less reading the papers. This was another strategy for grading: don't read any of them and give all A's. Who would complain about the lack of feedback in the face of an easy A?

She handed me a paper, face down. "Coco, what are the instructions? I can't tell if you're on the right track or not from what you're telling me."

I gave a Cheshire grin to show my appreciation as Yvette, talking on the phone, waved an absent goodbye. I mouthed a thank you and got up, leaving her to the conversation with her daughter that I could still hear from my office across the hall.

Chapter Ten

Wednesday Afternoon

Behind my desk, I started reading. At the beginning of the process recording was a required narrative to set up the who, what, where, and when of the helping situation, followed by reconstructed dialogue, written in playwright style. Emily wrote that, still having doubts about Siobhan's suicide, she'd gone to the Narcotics unit and asked there about Zach, Siobhan's boyfriend, the supposed drug dealer. But she only had the first name.

Interesting that Emily had been forthright on her motives. She'd probably learned from her previous submission that Yvette didn't read them, just checked off whether they were completed.

A detective apparently emerged from the cubicles, the only person there. I visualized a layout similar to that of Homicide. Emily referred to the detective as "Dev." To maintain confidentiality, we always used disguised names. "Dev" claimed to know to whom she was referring, but she had to come with him to check it out. I continued to read the dialogue Emily had written.

Dev: You're with me if anyone asks. I need you on one of my cases. It's true—it sounds like you have good information. Obviously, you work out. What do you do?

Intern: Walking, free weights, stuff like that.

Dev: You should work out with me at the police gym. Not that you don't look good already . . . Where to?

Intern: Can't we drive down to where he works, check it out?

Dev: We can't just show up there. That'll blow our cover. I've got to fill you in first. The way it works in Narcotics is you find your own cases. Citizens call up, and then you see if there's anything to it. Then you might infiltrate the suspects, start going in, and make friends.

Intern: But don't they know you're police?

Dev (laughs): This is not my only look, Emily. I grow out my hair down to about here. I wear tight jeans with holes in them. You'd like it... What's the guy's last name again?

Intern: I told you. I don't know. His name is Zach. He was Siobhan Weaver's boyfriend. I guess he works out of a restaurant. They said it was suicide, but he might have killed her.

Dev: Oh, sure, that narrows it down.

Intern: I'm here because you said you knew who he was.

Dev: I never said that.

Intern: You said he was your case.

Dev: Did anyone ever tell you how cute you look when you blush, Emily?

Intern: You know I have a boyfriend?

Dev: I figured you did, an attractive woman like you.

Intern gives name.

Dev: Him? All I can say is, girl, you can do much better.

Intern: Like you?

Dev: Emily, you were so obvious, coming into Narcotics on such a flimsy excuse. [He pitched his voice high, imitating her.] Some drug dealer named Zach. I've seen this before. Girls who work at the police department see me in the halls and think, 'Who's he?' Then they manufacture some excuse to come up to me. 'Tell me about working Narcotics, it must be so exciting. Show me a picture of when you had long hair.'

Intern: Laughs.

Dev: What's so funny? You know what I'm saying is true?

Intern: No, I'm just wondering what you do with the drugs you find, and which could produce these delusions. You were the one who came up to me when I was trying to find out who worked on this case. You said it was yours and would tell me all about it.

Dev: I saw you eyeing me in the hall a few minutes before.

Intern: No, I wasn't. And I certainly didn't make up some story to meet you. I want to find out about this Zach and his connection to Siobhan.

Dev sulks, and intern feels responsible, but this might be a cognitive distortion that she is responsible for someone else's feelings.

Intern: You're married. You're not supposed to be going after other women.

Dev: Let's get one thing straight. I don't have to go after women. They come to me.

Intern: I didn't come to you. I was looking for information about a drug dealer named Zach.

Dev: Do you have any idea how many dealers are called Zach?

Intern: What would your wife say about all this?

Dev: Do you think she'd divorce me? Do you think she'd give up the house in Germantown?

Intern: Can you answer one question? If agents come to someone's house and question them about their drug connections, which agency is that?

Dev: DEA, FBI, one of those.

Intern: Not D.C. Metro?

Dev: Agents are federal.

Intern: What differentiates the jurisdiction?

Dev: Two, three kilos, anything over that.

I raised my head from the typewritten paper and stared unseeingly out the glass to the hallway. Wow, what a bizarre interaction. I wondered when it had happened. After I told her she shouldn't be looking into the murder, that she should focus on the internship? Did she instead go off to find out more? She already knew the first name of the guy she was after; perhaps Siobhan had mentioned his name when they talked.

In search of a sergeant in Narcotics who could have told her something about a drug dealer only from his first name, Emily was a sitting target for Dev to manipulate to his advantage. He'd pretended he could help her and then had lured her out of the department alone. Could Dev, the narcissist that he clearly was, turn to rage after the rejection? As law enforcement, he would know how to hide his tracks.

I lowered my head and put my fingers to my temples. I was galloping away in my mind with conjecture. What I did have proof of in her writing—sexual harassment: the accidental touch, commenting about her body. And he knew she couldn't report it. She had no business trying to locate a drug dealer. Maybe he'd even heard that she was already "out of line" through the police gossip line, another reason to take advantage. Had Sergeant Bronson become aware of her going to Narcotics? He hadn't mentioned it as a further reason for her firing, but it certainly added to the case. Emily *had* been obsessed.

It was time to revisit the police department. Neither Kaitlin nor Anita had responded to my attempts to reach them. On my computer screen, an email had come in from Peter Vinter. He'd found the business cards of her healthcare providers—a psychiatrist and a therapist—that they'd found in her wallet in her coat pocket. Having taken care of the co-pays, Emily had handled it all herself.

On a Google search, I found the psychiatrist Dr. Leven's name on various listings, such as My Provider, but he didn't have a website. Not that it was unusual. Psychiatrists, especially those who took insurance, didn't need to advertise. The lighting on the black and white headshot hinted at times long ago.

On Dr. Leven's answering machine, a man's voice wheezed that he was taking new clients and to leave a message. Psychiatrists in private practice managed their own appointments to avoid the expense of a calling service or receptionist. As a result, many let voice mails languish without reply and refused email because it was not HIPAA compliant. I was prepping in my head the message to leave when *this voicemail box is full* rang in my ear.

Turning to the computer, I pulled up the therapist's group practice, Tranquil Peace. On their website was a photo of Theodore "Ted" Hodgkin. He was a distinguished older man with soft white hair and bright blue eyes, shamelessly played up by a matching Oxford shirt. I left a message saying I had some important information about his client, Emily Vinter.

When I hung up the phone, I thought more about how I was going to talk to Dr. Leven. *Another* trip to D.C.? An email from Seth pinged on my desktop. I'd succeeded in diverting Barbara from the rice diet. His mother was flying from Miami to Reagan National in five days. I smiled at the prospect of my announcement to the kids. *Grammy's coming again*!

The last time I'd said this, Noah, the cheeky little thing, took out his pacifier and said, *Grammy buy me guys*. We called his action figures, *guys*. Sometimes, he liked to sort them; mostly, he liked to throw them across the room to see which of them landed further.

The front walls of our offices were glass, lining the hallways. I faced out behind my desk so I could see who was going by and no one could sneak up and startle me. Catching sight of a blur of movement behind my monitor, I saw Maddy's iron-flat blonde hair whipping past.

"Maddy!" I called out from behind my desk, half-rising. She was just the person I wanted to talk to after Lissa's confession.

Maddy ducked into Yvette's office, but Yvette would have none of it. "Maddy, Dr. Knight is talking to you. You need to respond to her before we meet." Yvette was one of those people who had a manner of authority—except with her own daughter.

Red-faced, Maddy appeared at my doorway. I gestured at the chair.

She shook her head, her long hair falling over her face like a teenager.

"I'll be quick, then," I said. "I heard there was a disagreement in your clinical class last semester about the group project you worked on with Emily." I avoided direct accusations and paused to see what she'd fill in.

Her blue eyes were bold rather than embarrassed. "That was last semester, over and done with." She made a chopping motion in the air. "We all got the same grade because Dr. Barker-Rufus knew we deserved it. I'm sorry what happened with Emily, but she wouldn't let it go, like OCD or something. She got her A."

"Her parents mentioned you by name," I repeated.

"People always want someone to blame when someone kills themselves, but I'm not going to play the scapegoat."

My eyes widened with surprise at the strong reaction. It certainly wasn't very social-worky. Maddy's eyes were also round—with outrage. I'd seen that look before whenever I dared discuss an assignment.

Scapegoating. I hated when students learned a concept in class, only to apply it to themselves as victims.

"Your little favorite wasn't as good as you thought," she said with a sneer.

No fair! I took great pains not to cultivate favorites and deflected any suck-ups. Perhaps Maddy confused a "favorite" with a student who was prepared and tried to learn.

"We could also say you put too much pressure on her to do a whole research project on her own." Her blue eyes were frosty as she spoke. "You could be blamed just as much as you're blaming me."

This wasn't the first time I'd been on the receiving end of an indignant student, and I hated conflict as much as the next social worker. "I'm not blaming you."

"It's against the law to blackmail someone." She thrust her thumb at her chest. "That's what she was doing to me."

I had to laugh at the dramatic phrasing. "Over what?"

"Emily said she would complain to Dr. Schwartz about how the group project was graded. If he didn't do anything, she would take it up to the dean if she had to. I couldn't afford another C. My GPA would have gone below a 3.0." At that point, students were out.

"So, what did she want?" I prompted.

Maddy shoved her hair behind her ears. "Something from a medical record."

Sharing confidential information from a record was against HIPPA and the National Association of Social Workers' ethical code. But so was blackmail.

Maddy read my reaction of surprise that Emily would do such a thing. "So, she wasn't all that you thought."

Caught off guard, I became official. "Emily thought a woman she worked with had been killed, not that she died by suicide."

Maddy nodded. "She told me that much. She said she felt she had an ethical responsibility to pursue it because no one stood up for a marginalized, mentally ill woman." She shook her head. "Obviously, Emily was rationalizing."

"Maybe," I said. "Look, you won't get in trouble. Not from me. And I can find another way to corroborate the information." I had no way of promising that, of course. "It's mainly for the parents."

That angle worked. Maddie would reveal what she knew, but then couldn't be held accountable. "Did you take a picture on your phone?" I asked.

"No, she didn't want any evidence. I put it in my notes."

I pulled my face into its habitual poker shape, but *wow*, I'd not expected this level of deviousness from Emily. "Do you have it on you now?"

Studying Maddy closely as she weighed her options, I saw freckles I hadn't noticed before under expert layers of foundation, primer, BB cream, moisturizer, and whatever else was currently required. She was mainly worried about getting in trouble, so I tried to reassure her. "Look, Emily's parents did mention you. But if you help us, it might lead in a more productive direction. She was obviously looking into something."

She frowned, trying to play it cool. "It was just a pregnant woman's ER visit. I copied the note and gave it to her."

"Come on," I said. "You must have saved something, so you would have something on Emily if it went sideways." I added, "I'll take total responsibility for this if you give it to me."

"Fine." Maddie plopped her backpack on the chair that she'd resisted sitting in. She flipped her hair back before diving in, yanking on a spiral notebook. Her hand trembled slightly as she flipped through pages covered in her bubble gum print and ripped it out of her notebook. "Take it," she said. "It's your problem now."

She jammed the notebook in her backpack. "Can I go now?" Without waiting for an answer, she went left instead of across the hall to Yvette.

"Lord, what was that all about?" Yvette called.

Had she overheard? But I could only hear her when she was shouting at her daughter, not when she was meeting with students.

"Oh, you know how they get with research," I called back in a surprisingly jovial tone.

She answered in a similar bland voice, "Better you than me," and I hoped we could leave it at that. I was eager to get to Maddy's bubble gum writing.

The medical language was laborious:

On 1/22, Veronica Naylor, a 34-year-old gravida 3 para 2 Caucasian woman, presents to the ER at 28 weeks with a chief complaint of decreased fetal movements for the last 48 hours and mild cramping with associated spotting for the past 12 hours. She denies any premature rupture of membranes. According to the patient, her obstetrical care to date has been unremarkable, except mild bleeding in the first trimester of her second pregnancy that resolved spontaneously. Her 2 previous pregnancies went to term, and she denies history of premature labor.

In the process recording, Emily had described wandering into the Narcotics debacle because she didn't know the last name of Zach, the drug dealer. Maybe there was some story about an ER visit that was supposed to be an alibi. Maddie was directed to look up the record for a pregnant woman who came on Sunday night. Given the date that Siobhan died, the hospital visit was a match. Emily had discovered the full name of Zach Naylor. Was that why she had died? Because she'd tracked him down?

Chapter Eleven

Thursday Morning

The next day, after preschool drop-off, I drove to D.C. It took a half dozen loops, but I finally located parking in a residential neighborhood in Friendship Heights behind Wisconsin. From there, I set out on foot to Dr. Leven's office. I had tried to reach him by phone but only got a full voicemail. So, instead, I decided to catch him in person, tell him the news of Emily's death, and see what I could find out from him.

I climbed to the second floor and found his suite. The door was unlocked so that patients could let themselves in. The floor squeaked underneath as I surveyed a minuscule waiting area, sparsely furnished with only two folding chairs. I didn't hear any muffled voices behind the closed door that would indicate a session was in progress. A white noise machine on the floor next to my chair sat silent.

As I waited, I forced myself to read one of the student papers in my bag. Not that it helped my evaluations, but I tried to get papers returned within the week of receiving them. I looked up. Hurrah, one done, and only fourteen more papers to go! I started on another one, reminding myself not to get lost in grammar and stick to the big picture, but I kept stumbling on commas and run-on sentences before I gave up. Most psychiatrists had fifteen-minute medication check appointments. It was over thirty minutes, so I rapped softly on the door. When there was no answer, I used my knuckles.

Still no answer, so I turned the knob. "Dr. Leven?" I opened the door a crack and then wider.

Books and papers overflowed from towering shelves and sprouted in piles from the desk and floor. A version of hoarding, of course.

"Dr. Leven?" I called again and waited. "Are you here?"

I took in a sharp inhale, loud in the silence. At the desk sat a man whom I presumed was Dr. Leven. He was slumped forward in his chair with his head on his desk. A chill stood in the air, and I suspected he was dead before I got closer and saw his staring blank eyes.

Backing up, I plunged my hand into my bag and pulled out my phone to dial emergency.

They would be here in a few minutes, so this was the only chance I had to find out more. This was the third death in this case. I moved closer, holding my breath, and checked out his desk, which was covered in papers and files.

A letter from the landlord lay next to his head with its thinning gray hairs. Dr. Leven was past due on rent at this building, and the letter served as a warning of eviction. He had written last names in shaky capitals on the Manilla folders in stacks. Clinical providers were supposed to lock up their files to keep client information private.

A siren wailed in the distance. I moved out of the room, down the hall, and to the outside stairway. Seth had called while I was in Dr. Leven's office.

"I found another dead body," I announced when he picked up the phone. "Emily's psychiatrist." When he gasped, I reassured him. "Don't worry, I'm fine."

"The thing is, I can't leave and keep you company. I've got a call that's about to start with a group of defense lawyers."

"That's okay, I didn't expect that," I said. "I'll just wait until the detective gets here."

When I hung up the phone, the patrol car pulled up, then futile ambulance, and the hasty conclusion: natural death, probably a heart attack. Now, a black police-issue SUV pulled up behind the other emergency vehicles on Wisconsin Avenue.

Sergeant Reynolds heaved herself out as if she was still pregnant and strolled toward the building. When she caught sight of me standing in front, she stopped. "You've got to be kidding me! Why do you keep turning up at my scenes?"

In my mind, *I* was the wrong variable to blame. There was another explanation. "Because these deaths must be connected."

Ignoring what I'd said, Sergeant Reynolds gestured to the stairs. "Up there?"

I nodded, and as I followed, she said, "You stay out here."

"I was the one to discover . . ." The image of him slumped over rose into my mind again. "He was a psychiatrist. Both Emily Vinter and Siobhan Weaver were his patients."

She stopped a few steps up. "The second name I'm not interested in. Not my case. I don't interfere with the other sergeants' business, and they don't get into mine. Something you haven't learned yet." She scowled. "What were you doing here anyway?"

"I was trying to help the parents, tell Dr. Leven that his patient was dead. That's all they need—to navigate the mental health system now."

She cocked her head. "You couldn't have called?"

"His voicemail was full."

When Sergeant Reynolds went to his office, I decided to do a little sleuthing on the ground floor within the fifteen minutes or so I estimated she would be inside the psychiatrist's office. The sign outside the building indicated some psychotherapist and MD names, a title company, and an insurance office. The psychotherapy offices had locked front doors, and no one answered my knocks, so I figured they had yet to be in that day. At the insurance company, an Asian woman about my age asked if she could help me. I asked if she knew the older man who worked upstairs, Dr. Leven.

She nodded and spoke in broken sentences. "He there for long time. Here before me."

"I'm sorry to say that he died—in his office this morning."

She put her hand to her mouth. "Oh no!"

"Did you see anything earlier or hear anything strange?" I asked.

She kept her hand to her mouth; her question came out muffled. "You found him?" When I nodded, she lowered her hand and said, "I do not see who goes upstairs. I am down here." She mimed poring over documents on her desk.

"Thank you. Let the police know if you think of something."

I moved on to the title company, where a woman with hair extensions to her waist and a flawless mask of makeup was puttering around file cabinets. She wore a vibrant red pantsuit that gave cheer to this dark day. I made the same speech as I had in the insurance company.

She said, "That's too bad. "I think some people went up there today, I assumed patients."

"Male, female?"

She shook her head. "Sorry, I try not to notice the patients that go up there. I know they have private business."

There didn't seem to be anybody else to question on the ground floor, so I sat on the step to wait for Sergeant Reynolds to finish. Three papers later, I was cold and impatient when Sergeant Reynolds emerged from Dr. Leven's suite.

As she descended the stairs toward me, she said, "If I'm still working when I'm his age, shoot me." I stood as she reached me at the bottom. "I'm sorry, girl, I know you're looking for some excitement. Must get boring in the suburbs, sitting at your computer, taking care of those students."

She had honed in on a weakness. I wouldn't have called what I did *boring* . . . maybe *tedious*? Most of my work required concentration and was done alone. I had three colleagues, professors who only came in on days they taught. I saw my students, of course, but even then, as a group and only for three hours.

Still, I had some valid concerns in this situation. "You don't think it's a little strange that three people connected to each other all die in a little over a week?"

"You don't know all the strange things I see in my job on a regular basis. Most of it you can't make up if you tried." She gave a thin-lipped smile.

I balled my hands in my pockets. "What happens next with Dr. Leven?"

She glared to make the point that my question was not welcome. She did, however, consent to answer. "His driver's license says he lives in Watergate. We'll make a stop over there. See if anyone lives with him, and then find his next of kin."

Watergate was the circular monolith in Foggy Bottom made famous by the Nixon goings-on. *The* place to live in the 1970s, it still commanded a pretty price.

Sergeant Reynolds was still talking. "If there's no next of kin demanding it, we're not wasting city money on an autopsy just to find he died of cardiac arrest. That's what gets all of them in the end."

As Sergeant Reynolds turned away, I hastened to explain. "It looks like Emily didn't just talk to Sergeant Bronson about the case. She also went to Narcotics and tried to find out Siobhan Weaver's boyfriend's last name." Sergeant Reynolds started to amble in the direction of her car.

I went on, following. "He was supposedly a coke dealer, and Emily thought he might be involved in Siobhan's death." I was trying to talk fast. "So, a Narcotics investigator pretends he knows who this Zach is."

Without turning around, Sergeant Reynolds gave a flap of her arm in dismissal.

I called after her. "He sort of sexually harassed her, and she documented everything." I stood on my tiptoes to get my voice to carry.

Her back to me, she said, "Not my department. Try Sex Crimes."

"What if Emily's rejection of him made him strike back?" I called.

"First, you tell me about some guy she's dating in the department. Then you talk about another one who's sexually harassing her." She continued trudging without talking, her back solid in a faux-fur jacket, toward the dark Explorer. I couldn't get through to Sergeant Reynolds about the danger that had caused three deaths. Would there be more?

* * *

After finding Dr. Leven and seeing how his death would be handled, I had some urgency about contacting Emily's and Siobhan's therapist, Theodore "Ted" Hodgkin. I had tried calling him to tell him the news of Emily's death and left a message for him to return my call, not wanting to impart that kind of news on voicemail. Plus, that would not yield any information from him. Unsurprisingly, he hadn't called back.

Ted's office was in the same general area of Wisconsin Avenue as Dr. Leven's. I crammed into a side street a quarter mile away, according to the GPS, with a Graduate Record Exam logic puzzle of conflicting parking signs to guide me. I snapped a photo for the court if I had to contest a ticket. Then I literally ran to arrive before 11:45, the earliest he would come out of a session, presuming he'd started on the hour.

In contrast to Dr. Leven's dowdy sofas and chairs that looked like garage-sale cast-offs, Hodgkin's waiting area was decorated in pale blue and florals, with wicker furniture and a bevy of throw pillows. A woman with a gray bob and blue-tinted glasses looked up from a

Newsweek magazine at my entrance and then averted her eyes. Too wired to sit, I studied the self-help books on the bookshelf and the business cards for the various therapists arrayed on a jutting counter.

Ted, taller than I expected and towering over a 30-ish woman in leggings, emerged at 12:50. He wore khakis and an Oxford shirt that matched his eyes, similar to his professional photo on the website. He wasn't as old as Dr. Leven but pushing up against retirement.

"See you next week," he said gently to the woman. "Take care."

She nodded, warbled a "Bye," and dabbed at her eyes before turning toward the door.

When I stepped in front of him and said, "Mr. Hodgkin?" he asked in a concerned voice, "Can I help you?"

"I'm sorry, I have news about one of your patients." I glanced at the woman with the *Newsweek*. She was still intent on its slick pages.

He took my meaning and gestured toward his open office door. "I have another patient in a few minutes."

When he closed the door, I remained standing, introduced myself, and said, "This is about Emily Vinter."

"You know I can't tell you whether I see her."

"I don't need you to." I paused. "I'm sorry to tell you this, but she died. The police think it was suicide."

A flash of shock went through his face from his eyes to his mouth until his professional demeanor assumed control of his expression. "Oh, my goodness, I'm so sorry." He raised his arms, then dropped them to his sides.

I nodded, accepting his general condolences. "Siobhan Weaver was one of your patients, too." He would say the line again, so I forestalled him by putting out a hand. "That's two of them now."

"Patient privilege continues at death." He said it so gently I didn't feel too chagrined.

"I agree, but if there's someone out there, and there's a risk of another young woman getting hurt—that's imminent risk." We were spouting different codes at each other. He gave me the ethical standards, and I was arguing future risk. "Please tell the police if you know who might have targeted both. Or I'll talk to them for you."

He shook his head, regretful.

"I'll just give you one of my cards," I said. "If you don't have their contact information, the parents' names, cell phones, and email are on the back for any billing." I had to keep holding it out to make him take it. "You might be in danger if you don't say what you know. The psychiatrist is dead now, too. I don't want you to be next."

This time, the shock shone through, and he didn't cover it up. "How are the police treating Dr. Leven's death?"

"He was—" How to put it nicely, since this was a white-haired man, too? "Older. The police, therefore, think that it was a natural death. But isn't it too many coincidences—first two young women die and then their psychiatrist? Three deaths?" I added, as if he couldn't count.

"What did the autopsy say about the psychiatrist?"

"I doubt there'll be an autopsy. If there are no signs of foul play, and if a relative doesn't ask for it, then the police won't authorize it."

"Okay." His voice was calming, and I realized he might have taken me for a delusional prospective patient who saw paranoid schemes where none existed. "You said I might be at risk. But what about you?"

Chapter Twelve

Friday Morning

The next morning, I headed back to D.C. After I'd left Ted Hodgkin's office building the day before, it had been time to pick up the kids. I used the receptionist's apathy against her, calling once asking for Anita, the next for Kaitlyn, so I didn't make the trip to D.C. for nothing. For both, she said, "They're around here somewhere. Do you want their voicemail?" The receptionist was too incurious to ask why I wanted to know if they were there.

Thirty minutes later, when I showed up at the D.C. Metro Police station and asked for Anita, the receptionist recognized me from last time. "You know where she is?"

I nodded, smiled, and headed back. Dead-ended at the corral of sectional furniture, an upholstered chest-high door revealed Anita behind the desk in a surprisingly large office space.

"Knock, knock," I said.

She took off reading glasses. "Come in."

I pushed the door open. "Sorry for just dropping in, but I was in the area. My husband works downtown," I said vaguely. "I thought I'd try to connect with you in person. I haven't been able to get a hold of Kaitlyn." Of course, I hadn't been able to get a hold of her either, but this made the point.

She bared her teeth in a strain of her smile. She didn't want me here, although she gestured that I should sit in the chair across her desk. Part of it was embarrassment. She couldn't defend what Sergeant Bronson had done, demanding that Emily be removed for daring to cross his case and the awful event of her death soon after. Emily hadn't received whatever was tantamount to due process. This was an educational placement where they had a responsibility to do their best by the learning experience, and they had failed.

She cupped her hands under her chin, all innocence as she gazed at me with wide eyes. "Kaitlyn feels terrible about it. We all do."

"That's why I thought we could sit down and talk about it. Is she here? You know us social workers." I smiled. "We do like our process and closure."

"In this job, we hardly ever get closure," she said. "We work with people once, and then—" She made a *pfft* gesture with her fingers. "They're gone. You've got to be comfortable with that to work here."

She was lauding what I viewed as Kaitlyn's avoidance as a necessary attribute for the setting. "I know we shouldn't," I continued, "but guilt is so common with suicides. I do hope Kaitlyn's not feeling guilty."

Anita shook her head, emphatic. "She's not, don't worry. She knows better. If someone is determined to do it, they will."

I stifled a groan. People don't want to do such a final act. They want someone to help them out of their despair. As a helper, she should recognize the ambivalence and tap into the part that wants to keep living.

"None of us knew how fragile she was," she murmured.

"No," I agreed. "Did anyone see her leave? You know I grabbed her backpack here, thinking she'd forgotten it. I thought I could catch up to her. Maybe she just left . . ." I let the sentence dangle, hoping she would fill in.

Anita raised her shoulders in her suit jacket. "Caroline wasn't at her desk. No one saw when Emily left."

I wasn't sure that Caroline, the receptionist, would have known even if she *had* been at her desk. "Any cameras?"

"They wouldn't pull the videos for this." She straightened some files on her desk.

I didn't know what *this* meant. A student intern? A suicide? Someone with mental health issues?

"How are her poor parents?" Anita clucked in sympathy, leaning back. "You know how it is; like me, you have two. You can't even imagine." She shook her head sadly. "You understand we couldn't work with the family. We were too close to Emily. We had referred them to the sheriff's office."

I nodded. It was the appropriate action to take so they had someone who could counsel them, offer support, and encourage therapy. "I think they want to understand what happened on Emily's last day here, though. They said they were looking for more answers."

Anita's face tightened with displeasure, and then she said in an artificial tone, "Of course, there are no answers when your child has died by their own hand." She put hers to her chest.

"Is Kaitlyn here today?" I asked, sitting back to match Anita's position. I had alienated her with my comment about the parents looking for answers, and I wanted her to see us as still aligned. "I was hoping to meet with her again."

"She's out on a call." Anita raised her hands, hapless against Kaitlyn's schedule. She sat back in her chair. "I'm glad you came down today, Cara. It's hard to tell you this, but we won't be able to get you the data."

I sat up. "Why?"

"After the whole mess with Emily, we think it's compromised, and we're not comfortable." She shook her head sadly. "I'm sorry, Cara. I know it was a lot of work."

All this paled in comparison to the loss of life and what Emily's parents were going through. But I'd spent years cultivating the placement, the research project, meetings with Anita, Kaitlyn, and police officials—all that planning and problem-solving with Emily.

If this would be my last time for a legitimate reason in the police department, I had to take advantage of my access and get down to further business. I pulled out the process recording. "I also wanted you to see this."

Anita took it reluctantly. "What am I looking at?"

I explained how the process recording worked and then said, "It's strange . . . it seems to describe her interaction with a narcotics investigator."

She folded her arms and leaned back. "Emily was really out of line, interrogating detectives."

"*He* was very inappropriate," I said primly and chucked my chin at the stapled set of papers.

"We don't have a 'Dev' here anyway," she said.

"We have to de-identify our work with clients, so she wouldn't have used his real name. But it's often close. For instance, Dev could be David—"

"We have a 'Davids.'" She enunciated the plural as if that was quite a different phenomenon. She shoved Emily's process recording across the desk toward me. "I don't know what her mental state was at the end. And I'm sorry, I'm not ruining a man's life over that."

Oh, wow. Clearly, you had to drink the Kool-Aid here to survive; Emily had not.

What Anita didn't appear to see, and I wasn't going to be that explicit, was another man who could have been a suspect. This guy 'Dev' was a narcissist. Could her rejection have sparked narcissistic rage? Or the possibility that he might get in trouble? Men like him worked the averages. If they hit on ten women, they might get that one desperate and vulnerable person who couldn't withstand the coercive tactics. And he had used all of them in a fairly short period of time: flattery, invitations, teasing, pouting, guilt-tripping, and baseless accusations.

"Whose decision was it to close it down?" I wanted to get at any other motivations.

"I can't get into that, but it wasn't one person."

I had gone too far in their eyes. I had mentioned that Emily's parents deserved to hear the events of that day. I had maligned their precious Sergeant Bronson and accused Sergeant Davids ("Dev") of sexual harassment. Usually, I was more skillful at calibrating my response, so I didn't evoke defensiveness. I had moved too fast. but the urgency couldn't be denied. What if the suicides were set up? Young female victims were often dismissed, especially if they had addiction and mental illness. The more I investigated, the more unstable Emily looked—the two-timing renegade boyfriend, her obsession with a dead woman—compared to the person I knew as bright, helpful, and quiet. Her parents didn't seem to have known her either. One way or the other, Siobhan had brought out a part of Emily she hadn't been in touch with before. Wild self-destruction, a deep well of unhappiness?

Dean Bingham's disapproving face with the phony eye wrinkles flashed into my mind. I would have to accept that my project was over, and this was my last day here.

When we'd finished up, Anita walked me to the door, with the receptionist, Caroline, sulking darkly in the background. But I had a lot to do before I left the police station—or was escorted out.

*** * * ***

After leaving Victim Services, I hurried into Homicide. Heaving open the door, I called out. "Hello!"

"I'm the only one here," a deep voice rumbled.

I recognized the voice. "Hello, Sergeant Bronson. Is Sergeant Reynolds around?" I heard a chair squeaking, then wheels rolling on the carpet.

"Nope." He emerged from a cubicle and trudged toward me. He wore his gun at the back of his slacks. I never felt like the back of my pants was a good storage spot for anything.

"Good," I said. "You're the one I wanted to talk to, anyway."

Surprise registered in his eyes. Then he gathered himself and said, "I'm sorry about your student."

I nodded. "Thank you."

"You wonder about some people . . ."

I quirked an eyebrow in question.

"Whether they're just too weak," he finished.

"Fragile?" I felt fragile myself standing across from Sergeant Bronson. He had to be almost twice my size.

He reared back and grinned. "Fragile—exactly! *And* no common sense. That girl's case, Siobhan Weaver, was closed. Suicide. We had a note."

Emily mentioned that the note seemed crucial for the law enforcement conclusion. Had someone exploited that tendency? Emily suspected the note was a reconstruction ripped from past diary entries. Emily mentioned watching through the crack in the blind as her boyfriend marched around on the phone before backup police arrived. *Could* he have been covering something up? Usually, you didn't have to look past a woman's partner to find her killer.

"Even her parents thought she'd end up that way, sooner or later," he said, switching his weight as we remained standing. "Girl had a great situation. She lived in a building off U Street her parents owned outright." He stabbed fat fingers down in emphasis. "She got free rent in exchange for managing the apartments. Do you know how little you have to work if you don't have to pay rent in D.C.?"

"That alone is worth hanging in for." I smiled to show him I was being sarcastic, then asked. "How did the call come in for her death?"

"Dispatch is how we get our calls." He answered in a tone of *Duh*.

"I know, but Emily said the officer she was with took a phone call, then went to the scene."

He pursed his lips in annoyance. "All sorts of reasons why that might happen. *If* it happened."

"He told her when she asked that he'd read it over the monitor."

He put a hand out to me. "There you go."

"But then she said when he went in, and she was waiting in the car, she saw him walking back and forth in front of a busted blind and talking on the phone."

"Could be getting back-up, talking to his supervisor, so what?"

"I agree, that would be fine, but when she asked him what had happened, he didn't mention calling anyone." Sergeant Bronson started to interrupt, so I kept speaking over him. "And then when she asked directly, he denied it."

He raised his hands and flapped them to his sides. "All I'm saying is it could be a hundred reasons. Could be he doesn't like being questioned." He pinned me with his eyes.

The warning was clear. He hadn't liked being questioned by Emily, either. Was it just the chain of command here or something else?

I posed another question. "Do you know April Owen?"

He smiled. "Sure, everyone knows April."

I laughed, pretending I was joking, when I said, "What does *that* mean?"

He looked back at his cubicle. I was losing him. I switched tracks, knowing I had a last shot. It was time to poke the bear.

"How do we explain away the victim holding the gun in the wrong hand?"

"That never panned out." Sergeant Bronson reached behind him and pulled out his gun.

I kept my face neutral, watching.

"See, that was my wrong hand." Sergeant Bronson said. "Let's say I was drinking one night."

That, I could picture.

"I might play around with it." He jammed his wrong-handed index finger into the ring on top and spun it around.

"Kind of like in a risky, *I don't care what happens to me way?*" I kept my tone light-hearted, though it was hard not to take it as a threat.

"Exactly." He cocked his left-handed finger at me like a gun and sauntered back to his cubbyhole without a good-bye.

If that wasn't an exit line, I didn't know what was.

As I pushed open the door of Homicide, I was aware of *displacement*, taking my frustration and putting it onto a more vulnerable target, but the IT guy, Ethan, certainly had a role to play in all this.

In a bold move, I finagled a ride on the elevator to the fourth floor from an unsuspecting clerk. From there, I marched to Ethan's cubicle, which was as stark as a Homicide interview room, where he was scrolling on his phone. The only personal item on the desk was a key ring with a car fob and two keys.

He looked up, then scowled. "Oh, it's you."

Definitely on the spectrum. "Well, I just wanted to congratulate you." I could feel my face growing hot.

"On what?" He rolled his chair out from behind the desk and planted his feet on the floor.

I kept my voice low, aware of the dispatchers in the area. "Getting out of doing what you'd been assigned—putting the family violence variables into a database. I know you kept stalling with Emily and that she even offered to enter the data by hand. She documented each of the times she spoke to you, you know. But you got your way, and now you don't have to do the work. She's gone, and Anita Ware has closed down the project. Congratulations."

When he started talking about platforms, interfaces, systems, and permissions, I held up my hand to forestall technical explanations. That was one of his tactics—drown people in technical detail—until they fled in sheer boredom or frustration.

"Hey, I have a lot to do around here," he said.

"Yeah, I noticed you busy at work when I arrived."

"People text me now to get help. No one calls." He shot a look of disgust at the lifeless telephone console in the back corner of his tabletop. He was totally *e*—no paper was anywhere in evidence.

"You know how much people's time and effort you wasted? And this whole thing—" I waved my arm. "Might have played into the student's death."

"How?" he questioned.

"Have you ever read Kafka?"

"Is that the guy who turned into a cockroach?" he surprised me by answering.

"Yes, also the one that kept slamming up into the bureaucracy at *The Trial* and the despair that engenders. Effort for nothing." Now, I was starting to describe myself, as well.

A click of a cane caught my attention. Not wanting any of the dispatchers to overhear, I shifted toward him and lowered my voice again. "With Emily's documentation, I could write a complaint letter."

"You can write a letter if you want to." He smirked. "It won't do any good."

"I write a very good letter." Even Seth the lawyer was amazed at my ability to get money back—from cab companies, even airlines—through the power of my letters.

"Fine. One of the assistant chiefs ordered it shut down." His face flushed. "Are you happy now?"

I wasn't sure of the purview of "assistant chief." It sounded like the "associate deans" that ran rampant in every academic department. "Well, it can't be Assistant Chief Nelson. He was part of the planning meetings and was all for the project."

Ethan's lips formed a straight line. "I'm not going to tell you who it was."

"Was *he* afraid of something getting out—about family violence cases, how they're handled?" I fished. "Why hadn't this assistant chief stopped the research sooner? Why now?"

He shrugged, checked his phone, and stood, and I realized he was much taller than me. "Sorry. I have to go to Auto Theft and do a software update."

I had no choice but to back up and let him pass. As I trudged my way to the elevator, pondering what he'd told me and wondering what my next step should be, a couple of the dispatchers, the one with the cane and another with an 80s-style perm, emerged from the bathroom, and we all loaded into the elevator at the same time.

"Now Scott, he's not like my ex-husband at all," said the woman with the cane to Ms. Permanent. "Scott wants to hear about my day."

"Not mine." The woman with the permanent rolled her eyes under frizzy bangs. "He comes home at the same time. He needs about an hour to decompress when he doesn't want to hear any complaining."

Mentally, I jumped into the conversation, offering Seth high marks, and called him once I left the building. My voice, as high with outrage as a student who had received a B, relayed what had happened at the police department, how the project was over, and no one was doing anything about these young women's deaths.

Chapter Thirteen

Week 3
Weekend

Doing our usual jaunt into D.C. with the double stroller, we headed to the American Portrait Museum. The only discipline Seth was usually on top of was *not to touch the paintings*, so Noah seemed to deliberately run into the David Hockney standing exhibit at the American Portrait Museum. When the alarm went off, Seth and I looked at each other and quickly walked off, Alyssa and Noah tearing after us.

In one of my hour-off shifts when Seth took the kids to Burger King for lunch and the play area it housed, I perused on the Metro D.C. website the variety of assistant chiefs. Unlike ordinary police personnel who were anonymous, the assistant chiefs had bios on the website. I had ruled out Assistant Chief Nelson because he had endorsed the research in meetings I'd attended. My bet was on Jim LeFevre. His bio said he'd served as lieutenant over family violence for three years, and none of the other assistant chiefs had that experience. I didn't know, however, what I could do with that knowledge.

Checking back in with the Vinters, I learned they were renting a truck and packing up Emily's stuff. Now that my research project had been terminated, I didn't feel the same obligation to the police department, so after preschool drop-off on Monday, I drove into D.C. to Emily's building off U Street.

Unlike the day of her death, this time, the front door was locked. That made me wonder again if Emily had left it open that day, or was it somebody else?

When I buzzed, the door released; as the worn stairs creaked under my feet, I remembered hurrying to find her. If only I'd made it up the stairs faster, maybe I could have saved her. Another, *if only*. And if I was feeling that way, what about her parents?

When Mr. Vinter called out, "Come in," to my knock, I stepped inside and noticed how scratched up the walnut wood flooring was. It was as if all the renters that had come and gone had carved their lives in the grooves. Light from the overcast sky didn't penetrate the windows, even though there were no blinds or curtains. The faint smell of the burner gas evoked the emotions I felt discovering Emily's body.

I focused on her parents. They wore their gray fleece again, and their faces were drooped. In the cramped kitchen, her mother and father worked side by side. They were packing the rice, soup cans, ramen—graduate-school staples that Emily would never eat—and putting them into cardboard boxes on the counter. The temperature in the apartment was frigid, and I folded my arms around me. Today, I wore a heavier jacket and my favorite khakis that unfortunately now sported greasy fingerprints from Noah that wouldn't wash out.

Noticing my involuntary gesture, Mr. Vinter said, "They left the windows open."

I was the one who'd opened the windows. I should have known the emergency responders wouldn't close them after they were finished with the scene.

"The heat was on this whole time," Mr. Vinter said.

"Isn't it bad enough?" A sob ripped from Mrs. Vinter beside him.

I waited to see if Mr. Vinter would comfort his wife, but he focused on wrapping a glass in newspaper. He placed it in a cardboard box on the counter—the glass he could preserve, but not his daughter.

I gestured to the sofa. "I'm so very sorry. This must be so hard. Do you want to sit, take a minute?"

As if she hadn't heard me, Mrs. Vinter, her face drawn with lines, looked at the bare windows. "What was that landlord thinking? Anyone could have been watching her." She pulled paper towels from a roll on the counter to use as tissue, wiping the rolling tears off her cheeks.

"Do you mind if I turn on the light?" I flicked the switch by the door, which activated recessed lighting. Finding its milky pall insufficient, I went to the floor-length lamp positioned next to a boxy beige sofa and leaned over to twist the button. Dust motes floated in the beams coming down.

"She wouldn't do this to herself—" Mrs. Vinter's voice wavered. "Or us." She bunched the paper towel to her mouth, shaking her head.

I made my voice gentle and spoke slowly. "Have you talked to the detective?"

"She was apologetic," Mrs. Vinter said. "She said she had kids and knew nothing she could say would help."

Mr. Vinter added, "She said there was no evidence of foul play. And the autopsy results confirmed that."

I straightened. "You got the results back?"

"Someone called us this morning from the medical examiner's office," said Mr. Vinter. He stretched a roll of duct tape across the width of a cardboard box. "The official cause of death is suicide." He grimaced, cutting the duct tape with scissors.

"Nothing suspicious?" I asked.

He smoothed duct tape over the breaks in the cardboard. "Her temple had a bruise. They said it was probably from when she fell. She must have hit the coffee table."

I hadn't seen evidence of a bruise, but that might have been on the side of her head where she lay. Could it just as easily have been a blow to the head?

"Thank God she didn't suffocate," said her mother.

"Nothing in her system?" I asked.

The couple glanced at each other, and I looked from one to the other until Mrs. Vinter finally said, "Antipsychotic medication."

My mind flashed to the note on the legal pad I'd seen in Dr. Leven's office. I couldn't read what he'd prescribed Emily, but medical providers don't start with antipsychotics unless, as the name implies, psychotic behavior—hallucinations, delusions—was present. The other reason for the use of antipsychotics was to bring someone down from a manic episode. Emily had claimed the reason for accompanying Officer Randolph was insomnia. It wasn't a stretch to believe that might be a symptom of anxiety and/or its first cousin—depression, both of which were routinely treated with antidepressants. And when that didn't work, it was a months-long process of gradually titrating to the therapeutic dose. If that had little or no effect, another antidepressant took its place or was added, again, another months-long process. Sometimes, after all that, an antipsychotic was used for treatment-resistant depression, which meant, by definition, that four antidepressants would have failed.

"Did she lose her mind?" Mrs. Vinter burst out. "Was that what drove her to it?"

"Did she talk about hearing voices, seeing things that weren't there?" I asked.

"Never!" Mr. Vinter said emphatically.

I was aware of Dean Bingham's decree not to share unnecessary information. He'd already warned that I was at risk because of my teaching evaluations. Directly going against what he'd said was on a whole other level.

At the same time, I'd told Emily's parents I would call her providers, tie up loose ends. I felt obligated to let them know what happened with my efforts for Dr. Leven. When I started the story, Mrs. Vinter murmured, "Thanks for going to all that trouble."

I nodded, pausing to deliver the news slowly. "The thing is . . ." I cleared my throat. "He's dead now, too."

The Vinters exchanged a glance for the first time as I went on. "Sergeant Reynolds is the investigator on that case, as well. She thinks Dr. Leven—he was quite elderly—expired from natural causes."

"Won't there be an autopsy?" Mr. Vinter asked, unfortunately now knowledgeable about such things. "Surely they can tell from that."

"When someone is old, there's no sign of foul play, and relatives aren't pushing for it, they apparently don't do an autopsy." I recited the fact I'd recently heard from Sergeant Reynolds.

Mr. Vinter reached for a glass in the cupboard. It slipped from his hands and crashed onto the counter, smashing to pieces.

"Peter!" his wife shrieked.

My maternal instincts were activated. When any glass broke around the children, I shouted, "Don't move!" I now darted to the hall closet and found a hand-held broom and duster set, which Mrs. Vinter took from me. She shooed her husband, who stood helplessly, away. "Take one of the boxes with you. This kitchen is too small for all of this."

As Mr. Vinter passed me laden with the box, I asked, "Did you talk to the people at Victim Services where Emily had her internship?"

He set the box down next to the door with a sigh. "We just talked to the lady detective."

I knew Dean Bingham wanted any story of that day to come from Kaitlyn and Anita. But they weren't going to tell it.

I would have to get more direct. "I know you don't believe your daughter would do this to herself, so what theory did you share with the detective?"

When he straightened, dusting his hands off, he said, "For a start, those *criminals* at the police department."

Mrs. Vinter poured the shattered glass into the garbage can underneath the sink to punctuate the point. "Or even here." She gestured at the window with the brush. "What was the landlord thinking? Emily had asked him for blinds, curtains, anything so some pervert wasn't out there stalking her." She turned to me. "Can't we sue?"

"I'm not a lawyer, so that's not my area." We even had something in the ethical standards about practicing within one's expertise. But how could I allow Emily's poor parents to leave D.C. with all her belongings and not know what happened the day of her death?

Mrs. Vinter had turned to the refrigerator, disappointed that I couldn't help.

"What did she tell you about her internship?" I started with.

"Just that they ignored her. It was a clique there, like junior high." Mrs. Vinter reached in and pulled out a head of lettuce and an onion. "It bothered her—" She broke off and stood. "But not enough to—" She shook her head. "Never that." She made a face and threw the vegetables into the bin with a thunk.

I moved to the counter, so I was closer to Mrs. Vinter. "Did she tell you about a family violence call she worked, a young woman who ended up dying, supposedly of suicide?"

Mrs. Vinter glanced at her husband on the sofa. "She mentioned that girl, remember?"

Choosing my words carefully, I said, "Emily became quite involved. She confronted the detective on the case, thought the death was murder rather than suicide. As you can imagine, that didn't go well."

"We hadn't talked to her in two weeks. We would have tried harder if we had known it was the last time." Her face sagged in agony, and my heart constricted at her pain. The best way to help her, I decided, was to come clean. Didn't a parent deserve to know the truth?

"You said before she didn't have a boyfriend." I began.

"There was a guy a while ago, Ted," Mr. Vinter said. "He didn't have too much going on. She was always *helping* him, trying to get his life in order. We kept telling her, 'You've got to pay attention to *you*.'"

"We thought that making this big move to the capital was her way of coming into herself." Mrs. Vinter smiled at the idea, momentarily remembering a different time.

When the loss overwhelmed her demeanor again, I said, "Did she tell you she'd recently started dating a patrol officer?"

Mrs. Vinter looked at her husband, who shook his head. "Why didn't she tell us?"

"Did she usually keep you up to date on her romantic life?" I wondered if it was the complication of Jack Randolph's other relationship, or whether she thought they'd worry about the age difference, or the danger.

Mr. Vinter shrugged, and his wife said, not answering the question. "Did Detective Reynolds know?"

I tried to be more than fair regarding Sergeant Reynolds, since she believed all the evidence pointed in the same direction. The relationship might have played into her state of mind, but Randolph hadn't done anything criminal.

They were both silent and stood still, seeming to absorb the news. Trying to calibrate myself for what they could handle, I continued, speaking slowly. "On her last day, the investigator of the case that Emily was involved with"—*or had involved herself in*—"made Victim Services let her go that day. She and I were supposed to meet. I was going to tell her that we could easily find her an alternative placement to finish off the rest of the year. Absolute worst-case scenario, a student takes the summer. And I always had Plan B research projects for that one every year that completely collapsed." I was trying to let them know I'd done the right things.

But not so sure myself, I marshaled more arguments. Both Rochelle and I had met with her and cautioned her away, citing her role as a social worker and within the host organization. I had entertained her theories of murder over suicide. I tried to reassure myself that I'd warned Emily from taking it further. The usual advice was for the student to speak with the agency supervisor. But I kept coming back to the fact that Kaitlyn had been a hopeless supervisor—never there, canceling appointments, too impressed with her own self-importance to give time to Emily, who was isolated and alone, vulnerable, at this placement. I hadn't understood until now how vulnerable she was to the attentions of a charming patrol officer, who ran wild on the streets.

"No one saw her leave the station," I continued with the story of that day.

A sharp report of laughter came from Mr. Vinter, which he abruptly cut off. "Fired? She's never been fired in her life. Everyone—all her teachers, bosses—said how smart and reliable she was."

I momentarily cringed at the thought of making my dean the bad guy. After all, I had initiated and developed the placement and the research project, and then had handpicked Emily. Yet, I owed them the truth. There was so little else I could give them.

I gestured that they should come to the couch as I began, "My dean said any information should come from the police department. He didn't think it was our place to be involved." Once the couple sat, they held each other's hands, which warmed my heart. I hoped that they could unite in their grief rather than being torn apart by it.

We ended with me agreeing to help by asking the neighbors if they'd seen anything suspicious. However, I struck out immediately at the other apartment on Emily's floor and the two units on the first level. No one was home or at least no one answered—until I reached the basement flat. A man in his twenties with a wooly reddish beard opened the door.

"Hi, I'm a friend of the parents of the woman who died in the apartment upstairs last week."

"Yeah, I heard." He shook his head. "Bummer."

"I saw her around because we were the only ones ever here during the day—everyone else is in computers, finance, the neo-liberal machine. I knew she was a student somewhere in Virginia." He said it as if it was very far away. "Yeah, sociology—"

Used to this misnomer, I automatically corrected him. "Social work."

"Right, but she worked at the police department." His facial expression showed it didn't add up. "I'm an artist," he announced.

He must've seen my eyes flicking around his apartment behind him to verify this and said, "I have a studio a few blocks away. I create, like, sculptures, so I need the space. I also help another artist some days. He's, like, eighty, so he can't get up on a ladder anymore to do his installations."

"Did you see Emily with a boyfriend?" I asked.

"You mean a partner?"

"That implies a little more commitment than I was thinking," I said.

Even under the beard, I saw his face register surprise at my answer. He recovered quickly. "That's cool," he said. "Yeah, there was this police officer. Kind of a dick. Well, they're all dicks, white supremacists. He gave me one of those hard stares, like I had more than an ounce of weed here or something."

"Did you ever hear fighting or raised voices?" I asked.

"They made these old buildings good—can't hear a thing. When I've stayed with friends in newer places, you can hear everything. The walls are paper thin."

"They don't make 'em like they used to." Emily's parents had given me *carte blanche* to find out as much as possible from any neighbors. On my phone, I pulled up a picture I'd found of a class of police academy graduates from seven years ago, with April among them. The image was tiny, but I pointed out April.

"How about this one? Did you see her around here?" I was officially in detective mode. It was fun to play a different role for a moment. With children, teaching, and social work, I always had to be so nice.

He stared for so long, I thought he must know her, but he stepped back. "No, I would've remembered her." He looked at me and teeth appeared among the tangle of his beard. "She's cute for a cop."

I returned a smile, which he could interpret in any way he wanted. "Were you here the day Emily died?"

"No, I was at my studio. That day, I was jamming, so I stayed until after midnight. When I came home, there was a note on the door from the landlord that no one could stay because of a gas leak."

I wondered when the landlord had arrived that night, and whether it was worth trying to talk to him. He'd probably insist that everything was in order—not admitting any liability for Emily's death.

"Could I give you my number?" I asked. "In case you think of something, or you see anything else?" I didn't expect much, but I had to cover all my bases. It was the least I could do for Emily's parents.

Chapter Fourteen

Monday Evening

Two boxes of Emily's school supplies squatted in my entryway, minus the textbooks I'd left in the trunk for Roberto to haul into the suite tomorrow. The cardboard boxes were a dismal contrast against the giant plastic playpen that centered our living room. With its determined, bright colors, it looked more like one of the conceptual art pieces in Seth's collection than a child's playhouse.

I took Alyssa and Noah up to their bedrooms, not wanting them unsupervised and touching things when I searched through the boxes. I also didn't want their little worlds contaminated by the fact of Emily's death.

I took solace in the cuteness of a child nestled under each arm, focusing with open mouths on the pictures of *Fancy Nancy* as I read the words of the picture book. Noah, in a departure from only briefs, wore a two-piece pajama set decorated with kites across a blue sky. Alyssa wore fuzzy, pink pajamas that showed off her cute, short legs.

When I came downstairs, I announced to Seth, watching news in the living room, "We're up to four stories." I went into the kitchen for a knife to cut open the awaiting boxes.

"That bad?" he asked.

"Actually, they were pretty cute tonight. This" —I glanced at the jagged edge of the slim blade— "is for Emily's stuff."

He sat up straighter on the couch and crossed his ankle over his knee. "You won't leave them here for the next year, will you?"

I smiled weakly, recognizing myself again in Alyssa and her mess, as I went to the box and slashed against the duct tape so carefully applied by Mr. Vinter.

I was surprised that, apart from the textbooks, there were still two other boxes. Even if Emily had saved all the printouts of her papers and had a notebook and folder for each class, I had a hard time understanding the need for two boxes.

Tuning out the urgent and aggrieved voices of the TV pundits in the background, I examined the first stack of papers I grabbed. I realized they were the first pages of police reports in chronological order.

Sure enough, Emily had printed the reports in hard copy. She had gone against my advice, and now I was so glad she had.

I soon figured out as I went further into the box that all the reports were called in as intra-family violence or family disturbance. Briefly, I calculated how many reports were there. A lot. But still not enough for a one-year period of cases, based on my knowledge of family violence.

Next in the stack was a set of stapled sheets, logs that the Victim Services counselors filled out for their time and the case number. According to Emily, there had been several attempts throughout the years to digitize this record-keeping; all systems had failed, and the crisis workers had returned to the handwritten logs.

Below the reports, a blank copy paper was helpfully labeled in fat Sharpie, *Victim Services Cases*. One reason I liked working with Emily was that she was more organized than me. The following stack comprised the family violence calls involving the counselors. After this, I found one-year follow-up reports from both the Victim Services and the non-Victim Services cases.

Wow. This represented a lot of work. I remembered Maddy calling Emily obsessive, and now I could see why.

The last case, the complete file this time, was the police report of Siobhan Weaver's death. Officer Randolph's report used passive language for how he appeared on the scene: *Officer was dispatched to scene with a report of a shot fired inside an apartment.* In pen, Emily had marked the blank witness box in highlighter with a question mark.

I got her point: who had heard the gunshot to report it? Emily hadn't mentioned this fact before, but I wondered if she'd wanted to protect her boyfriend.

I thought about whether the Vinters had tried to access Emily's devices and maybe would work up to asking that eventually. Their needs obviously came before the dataset.

I briefly considered recreating the dataset myself. But the amount of time and the tedious work involved was unbearable. I had four articles in process and a book manuscript I had spent minimal effort on since Emily's death, as well as taking care of kids.

After I joined Seth on the couch, explaining what I'd found and batting ideas around, he said, "I think it's good that you're using more childcare, doing things for yourself, and not just focusing on the kids and work."

"But I shouldn't do that. I should spend as much time as possible with them."

"Cara, you deserve to have time for yourself."

I smiled. What a nice husband I had. Then he reminded me that I was supposed to pick up his mother the next day at Reagan Airport.

* * *

At Reagan, I threw Barbara's suitcase and tote in the back of the car and jumped into the driver's seat.

"Okay, what have you gotten yourself into this time?" Barbara asked.

I took a deep breath in preparation for the amount of explanation it would take for her to understand how we'd gotten to this point. This was why Seth didn't tell her about his office goings-on, even though she would like nothing more than to know all his business. I started with Siobhan Weaver as I maneuvered into the lane that would take me south toward Alexandria, doing a *do-si-do* with an Audi SUV heading toward D.C.

As I drove down the George Washington Parkway alongside the Potomac, Barbara turned from admiring the view of the Jefferson Memorial on the other side of the river.

"What kind of name is Siobhan?"

"Irish."

"How do you spell it?"

I spelled it while driving, like all the other traffic, twenty miles above the forty-mile-an-hour speed limit. "It's a pretty name. If we had another girl, that's what I would name her."

Barbara clapped her hands together and beamed. "Are you having another child?"

"No, Barbara, no more. Noah has put us over the edge. Plus, I'm already forty-four. We were lucky to have two healthy pregnancies." I said this so firmly that she allowed me to continue with the case she would supposedly help me with.

I backtracked to Emily's first meeting with Siobhan, how police were called to her apartment, and, although no charges were filed, the responding officer was sufficiently concerned about her emotional state to contact a counselor.

As we exited 395 South, Barbara said, "So you never met this Siobhan?"

"No, my student—"

"Emily!" She pointed at me.

I nodded and smiled. "Good job, Grammy! Emily was riding along with a patrol officer that night. His name is Jack Randolph."

"Jack Randolph," she repeated.

"They were dating."

She frowned. "She went out on a date with a police officer while he was working?"

"Patrol officers are allowed to have 'ride-alongs,' where they take along civilians on their shift." I decided not to go into the ride-along training aspect of Emily's internship, how she and Jack had met, and other aspects of the dysfunctional backstory.

I wondered if I should talk to the responding officer at Siobhan's police call. He was there when the mystery started to unfold. But it was hard enough to get a call back from anyone at the police department that I knew, much less someone whose name I would have to track down. How would I even start? Except for the higher-ups, law enforcement personnel remained anonymous and inaccessible by social media and the public.

"Siobhan admitted to Emily that her boyfriend was a married coke dealer," I said.

Barbara's mouth gaped open. "Was she a slut or something?"

"Grammy, we don't do slut-shaming anymore."

"We don't? But she was dating a married man."

"Let's reserve judgment for now, okay? The next thing we know, Siobhan's dead."

"Oh, my God!"

"They said she died of suicide—gunshot wound. But Emily questioned that." I did the counts against the wheel with my finger. "One, Jack Randolph got a phone call right before. He claimed it was a cop buddy, nothing at all, but she thought his mood changed after that to the point that she remembered asking him, 'Is anything wrong.'

"Two, Emily said that Siobhan didn't own a gun, and three, she shot herself with her right hand even though she was left-handed."

Barbara winced and reflected, staring out the window as we headed to the Edsall Road exit. "Isn't it obvious that it was the wife who shot her? This slut was sleeping with her husband."

"Grammy," I chided in the voice used for children. "Agreed, she had a motive, but boyfriends and husbands are always the first suspect."

She chuckled in recognition.

I picked up the pace of the story. I told her about Emily's death. I told her about April and the question about whether Jack and April were still together.

"So that woman has a motive, too!"

"Agreed, but I don't have the authority to find out where she was when it happened."

She cackled again. "From what you told me, she'd shoot you if you tried to question her."

"A tough cookie, for sure." I continued, telling her I'd tried to talk to Sergeants Bronson and Reynolds to no avail. I told her about the vial of coke I'd found in Emily's backpack.

"She was a coke addict, too?"

I shook my head. "She didn't have coke in her system when she died."

"But that stuff doesn't stick around long. What, like three days?"

I nodded, then told her about Emily's parents and trying to help them by searching out her providers. Even Barbara could guess the ending when I set up the psychiatrist's office. "Don't tell me he was dead, too?"

As we passed the Bowl America that served as the landmark for Edsall Road South, Barbara said, "You do need my help. I got up here just in time."

* * *

Despite supposedly wanting to help, Barbara had to take a day off after getting there to "rest". It was timed nicely with my teaching day, so I was good with it. On Wednesday, though, getting Barbara ready was much harder than with the kids. I outlined the plan once she finally made her way from the basement to eat breakfast and take her pills: after we dropped off the kids for preschool, we'd head into D.C. From there, we'd visit the scene of Siobhan's death to get the lay of the land and then make our way to Zach's storefront.

Pleased with myself, I explained how I'd discovered where he worked. "After Google led me nowhere, all I had to go on was that he owned a restaurant in D.C., and his name was Zach Naylor. So, I called like a million places, ruling out the ethnic restaurants, asking for 'Zach Naylor, the owner.' I started in Northwest D.C. when Siobhan lived there until I found *Best Barbecue* in the Northeast sector.

Barbara was less impressed with my diligence and cleverness than with the prospect of eating barbecue, one of her favorites.

* * *

In Siobhan's neighborhood, the same general area as Emily's, I told Barbara that Seth and I had searched this area for a rental when we first moved here. I admired the detail on the Victorians—the peaked roofs, turrets, and the decorative designs around the eaves. D.C. is known for monuments, museums, and politics, but not necessarily for its beautiful residential neighborhoods. After Texas, my soul thirsted for something built in the early 1900's. However, the cost and lack of convenience soon sent us racing to the suburbs.

Barbara made a face as she inched along the sidewalk, passive-aggressively slow. "This area's beat up. I'm glad you got a newer place."

I could hear the swish of traffic from U Street or 18th or 14th; I didn't have enough of a sense of direction to know exactly, but this street was quiet. Only a middle-aged white man wearing the hat and scarf necessary against today's chill passed us on the sidewalk. My fleece coat wasn't cutting it today.

"Can you make it up the stairs?" I called back to Barbara when I located Siobhan's building. Perhaps two dozen steps of wrought iron led to the front door. A bay window bulged out on the first floor. Amongst the row of Victorians on this street, hers was the most beat-up and badly in need of further renovation.

A brisk wind blew, and I folded my arms against my chest.

"It's too cold!" Barbara wailed.

"If you move faster, it'll warm you up." I was my usual several feet in front, my level of infuriation mounting. "If you go any slower, you'll be moving backward," I called to her, giving way to my frustration.

She flashed me a look, saving her breath for the exertion. I marveled that she became so undone by a matter of yards with no physical malady to account for it.

The iron steps clanged when I climbed them. I prepared myself for the ordeal of trying to get into the building and was pleasantly surprised when a click answered the buzzer to Siobhan's apartment. I grabbed the knob in fear of missing my chance.

I glanced around the foyer's interior as I held the door for Barbara. She leaned heavily on the balustrade as if she had just finished a marathon. I thought back to the broken toilet roll dispenser found on the bathroom floor after Barbara's last visit. She'd denied everything, but the thing had come undone from the wall, breaking off a bit of plaster with it.

"All right, Barbara, you're almost there," I encouraged. As I waited, I glanced around. The entryway had all the faded elegance of Emily's; like hers, the building housed several flats. I had argued against Emily's death as suicide—she wouldn't have turned around and done something that she'd just found so upsetting—but the level of identification with Siobhan was high.

With all the carrying on, an older man peered out the first-floor apartment door. Sergeant Bronson had said, as well as Emily, that Siobhan had managed her parents' apartment building in D.C. I assumed that this was Siobhan's father.

His bushy eyebrows lowered. "Oh, I thought you would be the man to fix the— Well, come in, why are you letting in all the cold?" He surprised me by speaking with a British accent.

I tried to forgive his crankiness. *Grief hits people in different ways*—a truism of the mental health profession. And men can get angry when they feel vulnerability. Plus, he was British, putting him into another cultural context.

"I'm sorry," I said, still holding the door. "I'm waiting for my mother-in-law to get up the stairs," I called down to her. "Barbara, the owner doesn't want me to keep the front door open." Finally, it wasn't only me exhorting her.

I introduced myself as he stepped out on the porch to join me. Sure enough, he was Mr. Dennis Weaver. He wore a navy sweater and slacks. His white hair was thinning, and his complexion was ruddy with broken capillaries as if he indulged in nightly bourbons.

"She lives in Miami," I explained, raising my voice so Barbara could take her cue. "She'd like to get an apartment in the area so she can see her grandchildren more often and so we can have family in the area." We *had* discussed this possibility, and I'd taken her to view several apartments. She'd even put a deposit down on one in Shirlington, but she derived a strange satisfaction from making decisions and then reversing them.

Mr. Weaver frowned, the tangle of his eyebrows meeting in a peak. "We haven't put out an advert yet. How did you know about it?"

"It was kind of circuitous, actually." I knew the word "actually" would help the man see that I related to him. I explained that I was an assistant professor at Virginia University and had this student, Emily, an intern counselor at the police department who had worked with his daughter. I offered my condolences at that point.

"I thought she'd end up this way. She'd tried before, you know." The words were bitten off from pursed lips that didn't open wide enough to reveal teeth.

I shook my head to convey *no*, I hadn't known, and to express sympathy.

"She took tablets once when she was a teenager. My wife found her on the floor. She put her back to bed, and Siobhan was all right then."

If they had just covered her up, literally and figuratively, I surmised that Siobhan hadn't gotten the help she needed. And now it had ended like this: the dark entryway, the chandelier, lifeless without its illumination.

Barbara, gasping, reached the doorway.

Siobhan's father told her, "I'm not sure it'll work out here if you can't do the stairs. Mind, it would do you good."

I flashed him a glance. Wow, sharp words to say to a stranger.

He turned. "I suppose you can have a look. It's not ready, though, fair warning. More than likely, the first of March."

"She's in no rush." I continued speaking for Barbara so she could catch her breath.

He looked at his watch. "The man that's going to fix the ceiling—you'll see what I mean—he's supposed to be here by now."

"This is a beautiful building," I said, following him in. "How long have you owned it?"

"About twenty-five years now."

"You ever live here?" I asked.

"We live in Springfield. Better value there—a proper house, garden, but we saw this as a good investment. We thought of moving here, closer to my work, but the renovation would cost too much."

Inside, the need for renovation was clear. The oven looked like it had been consumed in flames at one point, charred through even on the outside. Cracks in the plaster of the walls made it seem like visible strands of giant spider webs. A few chunks of the decorative cornice had fallen off and reminded me of a crumbling cake.

As Barbara gushed over the place, Mr. Weaver's lip curled like he automatically still cringed at the American accent. She gravitated toward the couch as if it was a mirage in a desert and plotzed on its plaid, scratchy-looking upholstery.

"Dora, where did you get to?" asked the man. "I have a mother and daughter here. They want to have a look at the apartment."

I didn't bother to correct him as an older woman in tights, a midi skirt, and a cable-knit sweater popped up from behind a center block in the kitchen.

She waved a scrubbing brush in her hand. "Oh, hello." She had a long jaw and a slight overbite.

"Oh, you shouldn't be cleaning at a time like this," Barbara said. "And those are such nice clothes. Can't you get someone to come in and do that for you? Cara has a great cleaning lady. She can give you the number. I don't know if she would come to D.C., but you can ask."

"That's all right, dear. We're not paying people hundreds of dollars when I can do it myself. Do you want a cup of tea?" Mrs. Weaver asked.

The whistle of a kettle made me jump.

Her husband said, "She doesn't want a cup of tea. Americans drink iced tea."

Mr. Weaver didn't want us to stay, it was apparent, but Mrs. Weaver couldn't stop the British custom of tea for all occasions.

I accepted since I hoped that would extend the question-and-answer period. The downside: now Barbara wanted tea, too. Barbara liked the idea of tea more than tea itself. When I made it for her, I added ice cubes and extra sugar; in the end, she left half of it. I gave a subtle shake of my head for her not to have one. But she bulldozed the request.

"Is there milk and sugar?" Mr. Weaver asked.

Mrs. Weaver opened the refrigerator. "I haven't gotten around to cleaning this out yet." She peered inside. "Oh, no milk. Just beer and yogurt."

"Then I don't want any tea," Mr. Weaver said petulantly.

"I don't know where she got this from." Mrs. Weaver continued to lament at the open door to the refrigerator. "I have such a well-stocked fridge."

"That's why jars fall out when you open the door." Mr. Weaver looked at me as if trying to share the jab about his wife.

Ignoring her husband, Mrs. Weaver said, "Siobhan was so thin."

Emily hadn't mentioned an eating disorder, but I wondered about it as Mrs. Weaver continued.

"I tried to tell her that if she put on a couple of stones, she would look much better, not like a stick insect. I told her, 'Men like a good figure.'"

Mr. Weaver snorted and turned away from his wife's tea ritual. "She had no problem getting men, although she could never find a husband. And how could she have managed if it wasn't for this flat I provided her?"

Mrs. Weaver clucked in agreement as she pulled out mismatched but brightly colored mugs from a cupboard to her left.

Turning to me, he said, "All she had to do in return was manage the building. But the people she'd pick! And then I'd hire people to fix things up again, and she'd end up in bed with them." He shook his head. "Disgusting."

I felt disgusted, too—at him, talking about his daughter that way. The social worker in me strained for some understanding. "You know, a lot of people feel angry when someone they care about dies this way."

"We're not angry, dear." Mrs. Weaver poured boiling water into cups. "She was on drugs."

Mr. Weaver seemed mesmerized by the steam curling out of the cups. "Cocaine, Marijuana." His interesting pronunciation here made the drug sound particularly salacious. "Alcohol, Ecstasy." He harrumphed. "The whole bloody lot."

His brand of parenting was heavy on the shame. He didn't understand that his daughter might have self-medicated after how bad he made her feel about herself. She might've found a partner who was not only married and therefore unavailable but possibly abusive.

"They know she had sexual intercourse that night." Mr. Weaver took a sip of the hot liquid. "God knows with whom."

Had Emily known this? Sergeant Bronson certainly had never mentioned it. "Do they know for sure it was consensual?" That was about as polite as I could be.

Mr. Weaver smiled humorlessly to reveal small, brown teeth. "You can't rape someone who is willing."

I sipped my tea to hide my disgust. My stomach cramped at its bitterness.

A buzzer sounded. "Ah, there's the man to fix the ceiling now, so I'm sorry, you'll have to leave. Write your name and number, and we can let you know when the apartment comes open, shall we?"

Chapter Fifteen

Wednesday Noon

When we were back out on the sidewalk, heading toward the van, Barbara said, "That was some weird shit."

"It sure was," I agreed, shuddering.

"Although a lot of it I didn't understand." She tapped her ear. "The accents. And that tea was the worst I've ever tasted." She stuck her tongue out and squinted her eyes shut. "The way you make it is better."

"You don't finish mine, either!" I exclaimed.

As we inched forward to the car, I tried to talk about the creepiness factor of the dad; Barbara kept coming back to the fact that Mrs. Weaver was cleaning, and in a skirt!

"Lunchtime!" Her painted-on eyebrows danced with excitement. "What's it called again, *Number One Barbecue*?"

"Something equally imaginative, *Best Barbecue*."

She cackled with glee at the prospect of barbecue, whatever it was called.

"Now, understand, we have to do surveillance first before we go in."

"But I'm hungry. You said it opened at eleven." And now it's—" She made a fuss of locating her watch face. "Eleven-thirty."

My phone rang as we reached the car. Of course it was Seth, now that I was sneaking around.

"Barbara and I are just about to get in the car," I said heartily. "We're going to lunch. You know those barbecue shows she's always watching. We're heading to a place on her list, a little rough around the edges. I don't think you'd be keen. Love you."

* * *

In the Columbia Heights shopping strip, a grocery store anchored on one side and *Best Barbecue,* adorned with a red neon sign, was on the far side. The dark-tinted windows reminded me of the two-way mirrors used for family therapy training.

I parked in a diagonal row of cars at the back edge of the lot. What was more anonymous than a beige minivan?

My commitment to surveillance withered in the face of the bleak, oil-stained parking lot and Barbara's pestering me about lunch. I was still pleased with myself for having found the mysterious Zach. But that was only the first hurdle. Now I had to figure out how to get information from a drug dealer.

I swear I wasn't hungry when I walked in, but my stomach clamored at the smoky flavor in the air. A man emerged from the back, wearing a black shirt and slacks. He wore a bloodstained white apron that partially covered the stylish gear. If this was Zach, he was taller and bulkier than I'd imagined. With all the coke, I'd pictured a svelte form.

"Can I help you?" he called to me.

I remained at the front door. "I'm just waiting for my mother-in-law."

He nodded curtly, and I could feel him glowering as I awaited Barbara's arrival.

When she finally barreled through the door, exertion had made her cranky. "Why do you always have to park so far away?"

When she reached the counter, she ordered willy nilly—brisket, potato salad, coleslaw, cornbread, the works. As she went on, I wondered if, when people came here for drugs, they talked code, like a *brisket sandwich* equated to a gram of cocaine.

"And you?" he asked.

I shook my head. Yes, I'd had to recognize that wasted food is a natural byproduct of children, but it pained me to also deal with it with Barbara. "We're sharing."

Irritation intensified, he stabbed at the buttons on the cash register. The flash of his wedding ring caught my eye, and then I saw the scars across the top of his left hand. I remembered the story that Emily had told, that he'd burned himself when Siobhan tried to break up with him.

Barbara paid, then stuffed a five-dollar bill into the empty tip jar beside the register.

He bowed his head in thanks.

"Do you guys have the best barbecue in D.C.?" Barbara asked.

"Sure," he said.

Barbara and I had discussed strategy on the drive over. I would start the conversation with how I knew about this place. "One of my students, Emily Vinter, recommended the brisket. I guess Emily knew your friend Siobhan."

His eyes blazed at me before turning to the register. He pawed at the cash. "I don't know who you're talking about," he said and piled the change in Barbara's hand without counting it.

"Siobhan Weaver?" I pressed. "You don't know who she is?"

"I meant the other girl, Emily. Yeah, I was acquainted with Siobhan. A lot of people were."

"You were seen at Siobhan's the night of her death," I said.

He held onto my gaze without blinking.

Seth claimed that when people looked away, they were lying. I didn't know if it was that easy.

Zach snorted. "Not like it's your business, but I was with my wife—at the hospital."

"Aw, is she all right?" Barbara leaned her elbows onto the counter, exhausted by standing.

"She's pregnant with our third child. She had some bleeding."

I hadn't expected him to be so detailed for a strange woman questioning his whereabouts. But if Zach had killed Siobhan, he knew a hospital visit would make an excellent alibi.

"When is she due?" Barbara asked.

His thunderous face broke into an unexpected smile. "March first."

"What are you having?" she asked.

I glared at her for asking such a personal question. I'd told her this before when she talked to random strangers about their pregnancies.

"Another girl," he said.

"A baby girl," Barbara enunciated with satisfaction.

I'd noticed that very masculine men tended to have only girls—a strange phenomenon.

"Will you keep trying until you have a boy?" Barbara asked.

I glared at her in horror. You're either in for another child, or you're not. But I had to give her credit. She had succeeded in smoothing the drug dealer's ruffled feathers.

After our food came with a different person in the all-black attire putting it on the counter—Zach seemed to have vanished—I retrieved our order and set it on the wobbly table. I sawed off pieces of various items to put on my plastic plate before Barbara could accost all the food with her fingers.

The barbecue smelled better than it tasted and comprised mainly of fat globules. The cornbread was dry, the macaroni and cheese too rich, and I wasn't even willing to try the dried-out beans. But we hadn't come for the food. We discussed what else we could say to Zach to get more information. Unfortunately, we didn't catch another glimpse of him before we left the shop.

In the car, Barbara burped and said, "Did you think he was good-looking?"

"No. Why did you?"

She nodded, smiling.

"Oh, you like the dangerous type, huh?" Of course, she had been married to a teddy bear, Seth's father.

"You think he'd boss you around?" she asked.

"Sure, the dealer's always in charge."

"That's what I thought." She stared through the windshield. "I wouldn't want that."

"Did you see the scars on his hand?" I asked.

When she shook her head, I told her the story, ending with, "If he did that over a break-up, what else might he do? Obviously, threats of abandonment make him unstable."

A Ford truck rumbled into the lot. I clutched Barbara's arm as I caught sight of the driver through the window partially rolled down.

Barbara turned to stare at me in surprise. I wasn't usually touchy-feely with her.

"That's Officer Randolph," I breathed.

"Emily's boyfriend? What's he doing here?"

"A customer? Hired protection? Muscle?" I fumbled for my phone and shot a picture of the back of his car as he headed to the end of the parking lot beyond the grocery store. I turned on the ignition.

"You're going to follow him?" Barbara grinned in excitement.

"Just to get a better picture." I stopped to let a pedestrian cross. As I waited, I put my phone out the window to take a shot unencumbered by glass.

When he turned right at the alleyway that went behind the store, I said, "I don't want us to get cornered back there. He's seen me before. It could be dangerous."

She shifted in her seat. "I'm kind of getting nervous now. I have to go to the bathroom."

"Oh, geez, okay. I can drop you at the grocery store." I turned left up an aisle of parked cars to loop around.

"Let me just go back to the restaurant," she said. "He liked me a lot more than you. I can get more out of him."

I stared at her in surprise. "You think it's safe?"

"Remember how I put myself at risk last time?"

I remembered it slightly differently—I had been in danger—but I went with it. "You have your cell phone?"

"Yup, in my purse."

"Is it on silent? We can't have it doing the *cha cha cha* in the middle of a drug deal." She had a particularly obnoxious ringtone.

"How do you put it on silent?" she asked.

I didn't deserve my phone, knowing little of its capabilities, but I could at least demonstrate how to mute hers.

After dropping her off near the door, I returned to another out-of-the-way spot. As I waited, my stomach grew queasy, trying to digest the fatty meat and worry about Barbara. I usually called Seth when I felt bad, but I couldn't this time.

Where are you? I finally texted her. *Are you okay?*

Trying to reassure myself, I remembered a time Barbara visited New York City. After a Broadway show, she'd visited the restroom and was so slow that when she finally emerged, the theater was deserted.

I had papers in my bag. I briefly considered grading them to be efficient and to distract myself, but I couldn't be calmed by work.

I reconsidered calling Seth and letting him know, but he would freak out and call the police.

With wild relief, I saw her coming out the door. I started the car and drove just out of sight of the restaurant. When she opened the door, squinting against the cold, I said, "Thank God, are you all right?"

When she heaved herself into the car, she thumped on the dashboard and said her first words. "Drive!"

I careened away, looking behind me, expecting Officer Randolph or his BFF, the drug dealer, to be pointing a gun at us. "What happened?" I said, giving her a visual check to see if she was hurt somehow.

"He called me a fat old woman. I should have gone to the North Carolina program, after all!"

I exhaled. "Oh, no, don't listen to them. They're a bunch of thugs. Can you start at the beginning, tell me what happened?"

She put her head back and settled in. "This time, the guy who got us our food was the one at the counter. I reminded him we were just there for lunch, and he was fine with my ducking into the restroom."

I tried to imagine Barbara *ducking in* but failed.

"When I came out, I just *happened* to go in the other direction." She could tell I was riveted, so was dragging this out.

"I heard two men talking. I'm pretty sure one of them was the man who took our order, Zach. The other must have been the police officer because the counter guy was still in front."

I glanced over as we waited at the light to exit the shopping center. Her lip curled as she assumed the persona of Zach. "'What the hell is going on? Some woman came here, asking about Emily and Siobhan. How did they know who the hell I was?'" Barbara leaned toward me as herself. "The other guy said something like, 'Hey, if you go down, I'm in the same position.'"

The driver in the car behind me beeped. Sheepish to be so distracted, I moved forward, making the left turn.

Then the police officer said—Barbara continued with her rough male persona—'These women. What are we going to do with them?'"

"What kind of tone did he have when he said that?" I asked.

"Tone?"

"Like"—I put on joviality—'These darn women.' Or, like, 'we need to get rid of these women'?" My patience had been expanded by having students and children. Barbara was testing my limits. "How did they sound?"

"I'm thinking!" she snapped. "There was something about a 'nosy bitch.'" She turned to me with a smirk. "I think that was you." Then, her face crumpled. "That's when they called me a fat old woman!"

"Who said that?" I asked, outraged on her behalf.

"I don't know—one of those horrible men!"

"Then what?" The G.P.S. barked another "slight left turn" instruction, which I missed.

"I heard footsteps." She mimicked with her fingers. "And I ran down the hall."

I cocked an eyebrow. *Ran?*

"Zach came around the corner behind me. I thought he was going to kill me, so I kept walking, and told him I was looking for toilet paper. That was the truth," she said. "There wasn't any in the bathroom."

Chapter Sixteen

Wednesday afternoon

Entering the heavy double doors of the school annex that afternoon, I felt myself settle from all the excitement. I had a meeting set up with two women from my research class who were older than the average early 20s student and, therefore, had paired up with each other. Melissa and Lily's project involved tracking violent incidents in a long-term institutional setting for people with severe mental illness. They wanted me to review how they'd set up their variables in the spreadsheet because they couldn't figure out how to analyze the data the way they'd presented it.

After I clicked through the database and asked a few questions, I figured it out. "Your database is organized by incidents themselves, rather than the people involved in the incidents and, more importantly, those who were not. Remember, one of your objectives is to see what variables—demographics, placement on the ward, time at the facility, and so forth—are associated with having violent incidents, so you also need those with no incidents as a comparison."

When we got all that sorted out, Melissa asked. "Is it too late to add whether their medication is injectable?"

"Why do we want that, though?" asked Lily. "We already have a lot of variables on medication."

I nodded in approval at Lily's question and her correct use of the term *variables*.

Melissa was unsure about her research reasoning. "Doesn't it say something about compliance?"

As they talked back and forth, my mind drifted. When I'd heard that antipsychotics were in Emily's system, I'd assumed a pill or capsule form. I'd searched her backpack and apartment, and neither I nor her parents had turned up a prescription. An injectable would explain the presence of the antipsychotic and perhaps the immediate impairment that allowed someone to subdue her.

But who could get access to both the injectable and to Emily, close enough to stick her with a needle? A medical provider? A pharmacist?

After my meeting, I began an email to the Vinters, checking in and asking if they were up for a call.

"Hi, Dr. Knight. Can we talk to you, please?" A small group of students stood at my office door.

I looked up over my monitor. "Class starts in two minutes."

Students were dying to meet with me just before class and during break when I wouldn't mind visiting the restroom myself. They'd lost interest by the time class was over, and I had the time.

Lissa, Maddy, and Naomi ignored my pointed remark and flooded into the office, thudding their heavy backpacks onto the floor. Maddy's face was pinched, and she avoided eye contact, presumably after our tete-a-tete over the medical record. Lissa took one of the available chairs. I reminded myself that Lissa was to be called *They*. Emily had alienated herself by using the wrong pronouns for Lissa. I wouldn't be guilty of the same mistake.

Naomi, a young woman with wild curls and self-confidence, flapped her hand. "I'm good standing. We'll have to sit for the next couple of hours."

"Yes, class is about to start, so maybe we can talk after class."

"We don't have any data," Naomi exclaimed.

"Oh!" This *was* an emergency. We were a couple of months away from completing the projects in time for the school's annual research symposium.

"I just talked with my supervisor about twenty minutes ago," Naomi said. "Remember the data that was supposed to be automatically recorded? There was a glitch. We have no data." Naomi's eyes filled with tears.

"What ideas does your supervisor have on how to rectify this?" I asked, trying to put the problem where it belonged.

"She doesn't have any," Naomi wailed. "She said the data's gone."

"Are we going to graduate?" asked Lissa.

I smiled. "Don't worry. I always have a plan B."

This particular Plan B involved Emily's project. After all, her last words to me were: I've *found something interesting in the data. Was there something interesting in the data to find out?* It would provide a ready-made project for this group of students to step into.

* * *

When I returned to the townhouse, having hiked across the storm ditch, I opened the door to hear Barbara saying, "Come down here, you little brat!"

I rushed through the living room and the dining area, where I found her at the foot of the stairs. Rather than saying *hi,* she sagged against the wall. "Thank goodness you're home."

"What happened to Rosa?" I asked, setting down my briefcase and handbag against the wall.

"They called her in to work the afternoon shift at the gym. I said for her to take it. I couldn't stand her talking anymore." Barbara put her hand to her chest. "Noah was a pain the whole time. We couldn't get him to come down. He kept slamming the door, throwing the superhero figures I bought him, crying." She turned toward the stairway and raised her voice. "Like a big baby."

It was much easier to empathize with Noah when I wasn't the caregiver. I *was* surprised he hadn't run downstairs at the sound of my voice and my clomping boot heels. That bad, huh?

"Grammy, we don't talk like that anymore."

"We don't? Then what do we do with a bad little boy—"

"Maybe we just ignore him," I said.

"Ignore him? He could get into anything up there. He's a two-year-old."

I put my finger to my mouth. "Shh, don't give him ideas."

She staggered to the kitchen table, dragged out a chair, and plotzed down in it. "I don't know why he acts like this," she said. "Seth never did."

"My sister and I were obedient, too. Of course, we were scared not to be in those days."

She grinned in a *you got that right* kind of way. "So, you can't spank kids now?"

I shook my head. "No, Grammy."

"Even if they deserve it, and there's no other way to get through to them?" She raised her voice again as I hustled up the stairs.

I knocked on Noah's door.

"No!" he shouted.

An invitation if I'd ever heard one. I peeked in. "Hi, Noah."

His face was screwed up in anger, with downward slanting eyebrows like my husband's. Such a tall and handsome toddler and so unhappy. He picked up his rubber Superman and threw it at the door.

I sat on the floor against the wall and picked up Batman. "Wow, look at his muscles. And how strong he is."

Noah watched me, drool staining his shirt, as he sucked on his pacie. I forced myself to slow down. I'd been going at full speed all day. "Is Batman friends with Superman?" I asked.

He nodded.

"Can you bring him over here?"

After thirty minutes at this pace, Noah allowed himself to be carried down the stairs, where Barbara was eating grapes at the kitchen table. "You wanna grape?" she said to Noah, her voice full of sass.

He turned his head away from her. I made a shush gesture to Barbara, my finger to my mouth. I didn't want to set off another round.

I eventually engaged him, with Alyssa joining in, with a game of "Horsey." Horsey involved crawling on my hands and knees while the kids took turns on my back. The *corral* was the carpet in the dining room where a table would have been for most houses. We kept it empty as a kind of dance floor play area. I crawled in circles around the corral, occasionally giving out protracted neighs.

When my knees became red and raw, I begged off, although Noah still insisted on being in my lap when I sat down. My phone rang, and I recognized the number as Peter Vinter's. "I have to take this."

Nothing can set off abandonment like a mother taking a phone call. Noah stretched his spine and leaned back so his head and hair were in my mouth. His goal was to block me from talking. *Oh, gosh*, but this was a sensitive conversation. I tried to struggle up, but Noah pressed downward.

"No!" he shouted, trying to grasp the phone I held away from him. I jabbed it on mute and extricated myself, trying to stand so that he would, at some point, drop away from his hold on my long-sleeve cotton top, stretching it to ridiculous lengths. Eczema was aflame on his angry face.

"Do you need to go?" Mr. Vinter asked on the phone.

I made a stern frowny face at Noah as I said, "It's okay. Go ahead." Noah glared right back.

I put the phone on mute again and bounded up the stairs with a sudden movement that Noah didn't expect. He pounded behind me as I rushed through the master bedroom and locked the door.

Noah began an ominous *bang* drumbeat on the door, so I fled to the bathroom and locked *that* door, too, in case Noah could breach the bedroom.

My voice was hollow in the enclosed space. "Sorry, go on."

"You said you had questions," he said.

"I'll explain after you answer, but did the autopsy find needle marks?"

He let out a gasp into the phone.

"I don't mean shooting up, like heroin. I mean, like someone gave her a shot."

"Like a vaccine?" He sounded confused.

"I was just wondering how someone could have gotten her into a car unless she was drugged."

"The medical examiner didn't say anything about a needle mark."

Meanwhile, Noah continued the staccato pattern on the door with something harder than his fist or foot. I could no longer stay in my confines for safety reasons alone. When Noah was younger, he'd thrown a vase onto the glass coffee table that used to be in the master bedroom. I hoped he had more sense than that now, but if he didn't get my attention, he might become unpredictable.

Despite my agitation, my voice was soothing in the phone. "People tend to blame themselves with this type of death. There's always guilt involved."

"My wife's not doing well. I tell her, 'You were a good mother. You were always there.' But she says, 'Emily told me who she thought I wanted her to be. I didn't know the real Emily.'"

I wasn't sure if any of us did, and that perhaps Emily herself was figuring that out. "Has your wife changed her mind about the cause?" I saw my face in the mirror. It was an expression I didn't usually see— one of sympathy.

"The detective didn't have any doubt," he said dully.

I turned away from my own reflection to focus on Peter Vinter. "Was there anything on Emily's phone or computer that gave you more information?"

"We can't get in. We don't have the passwords."

The line beeped. There was some law that I didn't get phone calls until I was on the phone with someone else. This time my cell phone read *Theodore Hodgkin*. "Emily's therapist is calling in. Let me get this. Shall I have him call you?"

"Just tell him to send the bill."

I hated to leave Mr. Vinter like that, but therapists only designated a couple of minutes to return calls. If I didn't get Ted Hodgkin right then, I might not have a chance until after the next hour appointment— or maybe never.

When I switched over and said hello, I pegged him as the type of provider who enjoyed the use of therapeutic silence. When he spoke, his voice was deeper than I'd remembered.

"I've consulted with some colleagues, and I'm not going to the police, but would you be willing to come to my office?"

Hearing another blow to the door, I winced. "Okay, yes, just give me a day and time. Mornings, please, after nine-thirty," I said, rather desperate. I hoped that if I pretended the noise wasn't happening, Ted Hodgkin would do the same.

Another long, thoughtful pause.

BANG.

"Everything okay?" he asked.

I forced a chuckle. "I live behind Smoot Lumber, and the trucks back here just fly over the speed bumps. The beds slam, and it makes quite a racket."

"Okay," he said, sounding dubious, like he suspected family violence.

Nope, only my two-year-old.

Another call beeped in—there went the law again. I hurried up the plan to finish with Ted Hodgkin and switched over.

A young male voice asked, "Hi, is this Professor Knight?"

A student? They usually emailed, not called.

BANG.

"This is Nathan Corrigan. I live in Emily's apartment building. I thought of something. You said to call if I did."

"Yes, thank you."

BANG.

"Are you in the District?" he asked.

"Alexandria."

"I'm working in my studio, getting ready for a show. Can you come out here? I want to see what you think."

BANG!

Under any other circumstance, I would've asked further questions, but I was worried about what Noah was doing out there—to the door and himself. "Okay, yes, sure. It'll have to be tomorrow, though. Tomorrow morning. Text me the address."

I hung up and ran out. Noah was in worse shape than when I'd first come home, crying, angry, head-butting when I tried to hold him and say, "Mommy had an important phone call. You can sit in my lap when

I'm talking on the phone, but you must be quiet." Of course, in his state, this meant nothing to him. It was one of his guys, Batman, that he'd been banging on the door. He hurled him at me. I dodged him, but Superman was next and hit me in the head with all his flying force.

When I finally came downstairs in as foul a mood as Noah, who was now in my arms, Barbara said, "What're you doing holding him? He's as big as you are." She held out her arms. "Come to Grammy."

He glowered at her.

"You need more help," she said, staring at him but speaking to me.

"You're helping, Barbara, and I appreciate it. Rosa helps."

"No," she groaned. "Someone who lives in and cooks and cleans."

I made a face. "I would hate a stranger hanging around. It would feel like an invasion of our privacy. And I made the choice to have children. It's my responsibility to care for them and ensure they feel a secure sense of attachment."

She flapped her hand.

"This is the modern parenting ethos, Barbara," I insisted.

"See, if you had someone, she would already have made dinner. We're having meatloaf again, huh?"

"Seth likes it once a week," I said.

"Do the kids eat it?"

I shook my head. "We strive for three out of four eating any particular dish, but we settle for two out of four. And the kids *will* eat the rice and beans we have with the meatloaf." I wondered if we should still let them eat with their fingers now that Barbara was here.

"Seth always ate what you put in front of him. He wasn't picky at all."

I nodded, having heard this before.

"I'll have a little piece. I like the way you make it. It's the best meatloaf I've ever tasted."

I was convinced that couldn't be the case, since she was from that decade when meatloaf was at its nexus.

"Do you want me to do anything?" she asked.

"You can chop the onions."

She held out her polished fingernails. "I don't want my hands to smell."

* * *

After I'd deposited Noah next to Alyssa on the Elmo couch in front of the TV and put the meatloaf in the oven, I returned to my computer. I pulled up the therapist's picture on my laptop and carried it over to the kitchen table, where Barbara sat eating shrimp and cocktail sauce. "I wanted to show you who I'm meeting with tomorrow," I said by way of explanation.

She leaned forward, inches from the screen, and stabbed her thumb at it. "Ooh, he's handsome! Is he one of your suspects?"

"He was the therapist for both Siobhan and Emily." I moved the laptop a little further back so she wouldn't get cocktail sauce on the screen or, worse, the keys.

"I've never had a therapist who looked like that. I would tell him *everything*." She continued to gaze. "Is he single? Wake me up at seven-thirty, and I'll come with you."

"You said you weren't coming out tomorrow. That you had to rest." The preheat setting dinged, and I could smell the meatloaf starting to cook.

"Is he married?" When I paused, she said, "Gay? Is he gay?"

"That's not what I was going to say, and I have no idea." I closed the screen.

"Aren't a lot of male therapists gay?" She dug into another shrimp. "Do you want one?"

"Not now, and no, not all of them." I pulled my laptop protectively into my arms. "You see, it took a while to get to the point where he was willing to talk to me, and he's still very skittish. So, he definitely won't say anything if you're there."

She plonked the shrimp into the sauce in a small bowl. "Those girls are both dead! What's the big game?"

"He still doesn't want to spill their secrets to the world."

She sucked on the shrimp, pulling the tail out. "It's not to the world. It's just to us, and we're trying to solve a crime here."

Chapter Seventeen

Thursday Morning

In Ted Hodgkin's office the next morning, I sat on the couch facing diplomas from D.C. area universities. The sofa was way lower than the chair across from it, creating an infantilized effect. I tried to welcome the discomfort, telling myself it was good to get a feel for how clients experience the therapeutic setup.

I'd been in his office before but could take in the surroundings this time. A bookshelf covered one wall with the usual self-help staples, classics on family therapy, and tomes of psychodynamic theory. Editions of the Diagnostic Manual of Statistical Disorders lined up together, perfectly illustrating how long he'd practiced. A strategic clock was placed at the back of the couch. That allowed him to keep track of time without giving the impression that he was clock-watching during the session.

We had agreed to proceed with first names. Ted shook his head. "Never lost a patient before. Nor two of them. I never thought I'd retire. If you'd asked me, I'd be doing this forever. But now, I'm not so sure."

"Come on, you're a pro," I said. "You've dealt with suicidal behavior before."

He shrugged. "Of course, and a few have gone to the hospital. But"—he held up a finger—"never involuntarily. I've always managed to talk people into committing themselves."

"That's what I'm saying. You know how to handle this. Now suddenly, you miss two in a row?"

He pursed his lips, nodding, and I sensed I had him in a better place to answer my questions. I started with Siobhan since he'd seen her longer. Because he was a fellow therapist, I dove straight into the suicidal business.

In answer, Ted turned his palms up in his lap. "Siobhan felt suicidal from time to time, yes. No attempt, thank God, while I was seeing her."

"Self-harm?" I asked.

"No, although she would hallucinate about a knife blade skittering down her forearms." He made his motion down his shirtsleeve as if he were playing a dancing violin. "I'd never heard of that before."

"New one for me, too," I said, although I hadn't worked much in severe mental illness. Most hallucinations were auditory—people heard voices, usually awful ones that taunted and berated—but, technically, hallucinations could be experienced through any sense.

"Did Siobhan own a gun?" I asked.

"She hated guns and their tragedy." His lips formed a stern line.

"How about her boyfriend?" I asked, unsure of how else to address him. The term *partner* wasn't appropriate when one of the partners was married to someone else.

Ted's mouth pulled down. "I wouldn't call him a boyfriend. He was married; she saw other people, too, occasionally. She tried to break up with him—over a dozen times in the period I saw her."

Ted had called me, I realized, partly because he wanted to process Emily's death. He wouldn't find a more willing audience than me.

"Do you think he could have killed her, like in a jealous rage?" I asked.

His eyes went inward as he searched his recollections. "We'd talked about the safety issues. One time, he was waiting across the street in his car when she came home from a date."

"Stalking?"

"I would call it that, although he didn't hurt her. He just came in with his coke and they stayed up the rest of the night doing it."

I wondered why Ted hadn't referred her to specialized substance abuse treatment, but outpatient providers handled that differently.

Ted put his hand on his upper stomach and grimaced. "But that's not what my gut tells me about who killed her."

I didn't like the gut. I'd been told by more than one social work supervisor, *just trust your gut*. I didn't know which gut, the "wise gut" or the "scared" one, that could be especially loud.

"Do you think it was Zach's wife?" I asked.

He shook his head and sighed. "Her father," he said in a low voice as if someone might be listening.

I remembered standing in Siobhan's kitchen and her father saying, *You can't rape someone who's willing.* I shuddered inwardly. "Her own father?"

"He was in the military in Britain—of course, that was long ago, but he knew how to shoot."

"The gun was unlicensed. Where would he have gotten that?"

He shrugged. "In D.C., they're available if that's what you want."

I had a hard time seeing Mr. Weaver making a gun deal with a street criminal.

Ted went on. "And he could've been drunk, out of his mind at the time. He's a functional alcoholic."

I recalled his red face and nodded.

Ted peered toward the window, where branches outside made a criss-cross shadow across the blinds. "She'd talked about confronting him." He shifted in his seat. "Not that I necessarily encourage that. Most people don't get what they want—an admission or an apology."

I agreed with him. The only reason for a face-to face was to speak the truth to the perpetrator. But perpetrators wouldn't say the right lines back as there was too much at stake to admit what they'd done.

"She wanted him to pay for her graduate school," Ted explained. "She'd gotten into an MFA program in creative writing at American."

I nodded since I already knew that from what Emily had told me.

"Her father scoffed at it, said if she wanted to write, she had plenty of free time to do it." Ted leaned forward. "She was always journaling. It was her main coping mechanism. She joked about having a whole trunk full of diaries."

The room was drafty, and I was glad I still wore my jacket. If Ted's next client was about to arrive, I needed to get moving on the topic of Emily, even though I still had many more questions about Siobhan. I told him what happened at the internship that final day, finishing with, "Emily supposedly ran from the police department to go home and turn on her burners."

"An old-fashioned method, very Sylvia Plath."

"I found her body," I blurted.

"Oh, how awful."

His sympathy elicited the emotion that Emily's death brought up. It welled up in my chest, then my throat. I swallowed the tears down and became businesslike.

"Emily was smart. She worked out Zach Naylor's name and his wife's."

Ted touched his chest. "I didn't tell her that."

"Oh, I know." I smiled, admiring her cleverness. "She even got some evidence that Veronica, Zach's wife, was in the hospital with pregnancy complications at the appointed time, a perfect alibi."

"A perfect alibi for whom?" he asked.

"Both of them, either of them." I shrugged. "So how can it be random that Emily would investigate one woman's death and then kill herself with a different method?" I swallowed again in memory. "The last time I saw her, she met me at the main entrance to the police department. I should've given her more time."

He reached his hand out. "Please, you can't blame yourself."

I gave a wry smile. The "what if" game. We all played it to mount control where we had none.

"She said she felt sick. Kaitlyn, her supervisor, was about to fire her. I told her that was impossible; our field placements don't work like that. First, we try to work things out with a specific contract and lay out clear expectations on both sides. She wasn't even getting supervision. No one would take her out on calls. I tried to talk to her supervisor, but they had already made up their minds."

The hands of the discreet clock edged toward the hour. Ted's face was arranged in sympathetic lines, but he remained silent, giving me the chance for an abrupt switch in subjects, the vial of coke secreted in Emily's backpack.

He sighed. "Emily told me she'd found it in the shirt pocket of the man she was dating."

"Jack Randolph." I shook my head. "You know he already had a partner, another patrol officer, April Owen. They've been living together for seven years and own a house. She told me herself."

He stared at the window as if the explanation was projected on the blinds. "Emily said he'd recently left his girlfriend. I warned her about being a rebound, but I should've known they were still together." He gave a rueful smile. "Rookie error. And now, after what you've told me, I wonder if he was turning on the charms after she noticed his suspicious behavior. Maybe he got more serious with her so that she wouldn't say anything to Sergeant Bronson or anyone else."

I was off and running on conjecture. "Maybe April, his girlfriend, even knew why he was doing it, to prevent Emily from talking."

"He thought she was a naïve intern." He cocked his head. "And in some ways, she was; she hadn't dealt with a pathological charmer like that. But he underestimated her intelligence."

I jumped to the death of Dr. Leven after Emily's. "I found his body, too," I had to admit.

"Oh, my goodness, you've been through a time of it. No wonder you're so invested."

I recalled Sergeant Reynold's conclusion. "Heart attack," I said.

"But in his case—" He paused. "It might have been the coke."

It took me a moment to grasp that he was talking about Dr. Leven. "Dr. Leven did coke? Was Zach his dealer?"

"Yup, in exchange for samples and prescriptions. Dr. Leven was Siobhan's psychiatrist first, but Zach jumped on the opportunity."

I put my hand to my head. "Wow, I was not expecting that." My mind whirled. "Could Dr. Leven have killed Siobhan?" I asked.

"The only way," he said slowly, "is if he thought she would expose him. He would've lost his medical license and been indicted. I wanted to report him myself." Ted's expression was more perturbed than I'd seen before. "How was she supposed to get better when her psychiatrist was not only an addict but a dealer? I consulted with some colleagues. The advice I got was that I couldn't report. Siobhan had to do it."

Yes, confidentiality over laws. That was the way the social work ethics worked, too.

The front door slammed again, and he straightened. "My next client is here." As he rose from his seat, he said, "Now that I've told you all this, I don't think we'd better talk again. You can take what I've said and do what is necessary. But I'm not speaking to the police."

Nicely played. He had put me in the spot of whether to tell or not.

* * *

It had started to rain when I left Wisconsin Avenue and drove through to the Northeast and Columbia Heights. More gang signs splashed here on storefronts with faded paint, and in the midst of an oppressively low sky and now a driving rain, I scuttled through an alleyway to Nathan Corrigan's studio, one of three similar, banged-up garages lined up in a row. I'd given up carrying umbrellas since I needed my hands for the children, and keeping track of yet another item was beyond me. Wet and cold, I stumbled over the uneven brick that paved the street and wondered how safe it was to meet him alone.

What if he was the murderer? He had opportunity as a fellow resident of the building. Perhaps Emily had rebuffed him; he'd become enraged, and set up the sick scene.

Somebody needed to know where I was. Seth came to mind, but I wasn't sure he would appreciate the younger man thing, and it would take too long to explain with a lot of unnecessary back and forth. I simply didn't have the time. Plus, Seth was the one who visited artists' studios, not me.

As the rain beat on my head, I texted Barbara. *If I don't come back, this is the address.*

When I knocked against the metal folding door, my knuckles, already raw, hurt. I held my hand with the other one and stepped back as the door rattled, shuddered, and eventually clanked upward. Even in the dim light of a stormy day I saw reddish tones in Nate's beard, which gave him an even more bear-like quality. When I talked to him before at the apartment, I could've sworn we were the same size, but no, he had a few inches on me.

Nathan Corrigan fancied himself a Jackson Pollock. Spray paint was splashed heavily over twisted metal car frames. As Nathan lectured about his "process," he stroked his beard repeatedly, a gesture I found vaguely obscene. It took me a moment to realize the metal scraps were shaped into the figures of naked women: breasts, heads thrown back, arms clasped behind their backs with—chains?

Seth explained that contemporary art pieces weren't meant to be "pretty" but to evoke a feeling of unease and tension. That was one of the reasons we fit together as a couple. The average woman would've come with her own style and insisted on it. This was all to say that I had a high tolerance for alternative art.

Nathan's eyes gleamed. He had seen the dawning recognition in my own. The abrasive air, polluted by spray paint, burned in my lungs. The water gushed down through the gutter and spewed into a strip of mud outside.

"So, what did you want to tell me?" I asked, moving this along.

"Can you show me the picture of the police officer again, the blonde?" He nodded and watched as I took out my phone and scrolled through cute pictures of the kids and Miffy until I found the police academy photo with the tiny image of April Owen. I handed him my phone so he wouldn't move any closer.

"I'm not saying I saw *her*." He pointed at the photo. "But, after you and I talked, I remembered a cleaning woman on the landing a few weeks ago. I thought maybe the landlord had finally hired someone."

"What made you think she was a cleaning woman?" I asked.

"She wore one of these smocks." He signaled over his own body. "And she had a bucket of supplies, rags, sponges, and shit. She looked like this person." He stared at the photo. "But thinner maybe."

"Hard living?" My mind returned to my walk with Anita, who had gossiped about April's messed-up family, the drug addict sister. Maybe April's sister would do anything for money or drugs.

"Yeah, like that." He smiled as he handed me back my phone. "The artist's eye, right? I can see these things. And, come to think of it, the hallway didn't look any better after she left."

I quickly spun a scenario. April, jealous of Emily, had hired her sister May to case Emily's place, and she pretended to clean. But Emily hadn't died then. If April had set up the scene, why the elaborate ruse of the antipsychotics and burners when a straightforward overdose would have been much easier?

Nathan broke into my thoughts, telling me about the piece I'd been staring at, my mind preoccupied. "This one's called Carla." Teeth bared amongst the beard hair. "I name them after my ex-girlfriends."

My heart clutched at the violence of the piece; red paint spattered over it, along with other glaring primary colors—yellow, blue, and green.

"Do you have cameras out here—to make sure your stuff doesn't get stolen?" I didn't know who would want it. I wanted him to know that he shouldn't try anything if cameras were recording.

"Yeah, we do, just for that reason." He went on to "Julia." Was he taking advantage of a supposedly nice suburban housewife, so he could show off his "art" and have someone listen to him? Was he that desperate? Or was there a worse motive?

"Well, they're certainly nice and colorful," I said, making a strange and random remark to disengage. "Thank you for telling me this. I will certainly let her parents and the police know. Now I'm sorry, I have to pick up my kids at preschool."

"Let me know if you want to come hang out here again," he said.

"Sure," I said with a fake grin and rushed out, glad to be free in the pouring rain.

Chapter Eighteen

Friday Morning

Hurrying to make use of the time the kids were in preschool, I was unable to restrain myself to an unreasonable twenty-five-mile-an-hour speed limit on Seminary Road, until a siren whooped, and a blue light flashed in my rear-view mirror.

My stomach sank, although I was grateful the kids weren't with me to see me setting a terrible example. When I pulled over to the curb, I trained my eyes straight out of the windshield and remained still. Although I had the privilege of not being a targeted demographic, police officers were jumpy these days. Mentally, I rummaged in the glove box, with its typical clutter and chaos of oil change and tire receipts intermingled with the registration and insurance cards. The only movement I made was to press down the window. Cold air swarmed into the car.

The figure that sauntered up surprised me by being curvaceous—a woman, April Owen! What the hell was she doing in Alexandria with her Metro police car? When she reached my window, my angle showed where the makeup ended on her neck. It was like damp sand from waves on a beach. April's hair was oiled into a smooth sleek knot, and she wore flattering wire-rimmed sunglasses. A pink wad of bubble gum was clenched between her teeth.

"You were going thirty-eight in a twenty-five."

I tried to look on the bright side. I'd wanted to talk to her but had no authority or the wherewithal to track her down.

"Sorry," I said. "Do you have jurisdiction here?"

Not answering, she said, "You got Jack in trouble."

"*Is* he in trouble?" The man had seemed impervious to trouble.

Gum gritted between her teeth, she shook her head no. "Because your story is going to change."

I couldn't read her expression beyond the dark-tinted lenses and decided this would be my only opportunity. My heart pounding, I said, "He was dating Emily Vinter, the young woman who died suddenly. You had to know that." Against the civilized landscape of the large lots that lined the road with their manicured lawns and wax myrtle, the scene with her was surreal, and that was before she blew a bubble.

"We share a mortgage, been together seven years." Cars veered around her. Round moon faces of drivers and passengers gaped at me—the poor sod who'd been pulled over.

"I saw him myself in a police SUV dropping her off where I teach." She chomped on the gum. "She liked him. A lot of girls do. She just took it too far."

"I'm sure your seven-year history means you know all his friends. Zach Naylor?" Her expression remained flat, so I went on. "Zach, a good friend of your boyfriend, was dating a woman named Siobhan Weaver. Siobhan died, just like Emily, supposedly a suicide. Your boyfriend was first on the scene."

She cracked her gum with impatience. "We don't talk about our work."

"Okay, good boundaries. But this Zach is a coke dealer, and Emily found a vial of coke in your boyfriend's clothes."

Her gun belt rustled as she shifted position. She surprised me by smiling. "If Emily had a vial with her, she was the one using."

I stared at April, wondering how to cut through her denial so she wouldn't slam my head into the steering wheel. "Did you ever meet Emily?"

"I saw her barfing outside the station that day." She cracked a laugh.

Emily had mentioned feeling nauseous from the stress of that day. If she had run outside to throw up, that would've explained why she didn't take her backpack.

"I offered her a ride," said April, chomping away. "She refused, but I said, 'No, get in.'"

She gave a clenched-tooth smile.

"Then what?" I asked.

"I warned her, just like I'm warning you now." She leaned her forearms on the window, so her fists were near my face. "Your kids are at the preschool down there." She stood and hitched a thumb back from where I'd come. "You don't want to keep sticking your nose in." She slapped the top of the minivan. "Anyway, Jack has an alibi for when Emily died."

"Who's that?" I asked.

"Me."

And that meant she had an alibi, too.

"Now you slow down," she said and sauntered back to her police-issue SUV.

* * *

By the end of the weekend, Seth, Barbara, and I had devised a plan to deal with April Owen's flagrant violation of her badge. We'd use it as an inroad. "Now you just leave it to me," Barbara said.

"What are you going to say?" I asked. "Is it going to be like that time with the valet?"

Barbara didn't have a problem with ugly public confrontations and sometimes told outright lies, such as when she posed as a wealthy matron from McLean or said she was from Coral Gables when she really lived in Kendall Township. Although, at this point, anyone at the metro police department would have deserved Barbara's ire, I didn't want to stand beside her when she did it.

We couldn't proceed with the plan on Monday since I had to attend our monthly faculty meeting. Tuesday was research class. Then in the afternoons, we had the kids to amuse. On Wednesday morning, I sent the kids downstairs to Barbara's quarters.

"Grammy, wake up!" I heard them call. Silence, then giggling—I imagined Noah pinching her or tickling her nose hairs, some torture—and Barbara gave an unfriendly roar.

When they fled back upstairs, Alyssa joined me in the kitchen, where I monitored the grocery store bagels, hard as plastic frisbees, to make sure they didn't brown past Master Noah's desires.

"I kissed Grammy," Alyssa said.

"Aw, she must've loved that." I smiled.

She shook her head sadly.

I didn't like Barbara disappointing my little girl. Don't sigh over my kid and then not wake up when she kisses you.

I complained to Seth, who was finishing his attire in front of the bathroom mirror. "I do need her up and at 'em," I said. "She promised to serve as my muscle today."

Seth smiled, always a good audience for my sense of humor, as he shrugged on a navy blazer. He eyed himself in the mirror. "She never got up with me when I was that age," he said and relished my subsequent sympathy. Thus mollified, he agreed to preschool drop-off, so I could focus on getting Grammy up and at 'em.

"Come on, Barbara. This is what you came for."

She finally emitted a complete sentence. "I want sleep." It was a little like the construction of Noah's first sentence, *I hit Baby*.

"You can sleep when you're dead." When I trotted out that old adage, she groaned even louder.

"You can go back down this afternoon," I cajoled, then leaned over and whispered in her ear, "What do you want me to make you for breakfast?"

Now I was talking her love language, and she started to rouse. "Eggs?"

I straightened. "Sure, how many?"

"Toast?"

"Of course."

"I Can't Believe It's Not Butter?"

"Just regular butter."

"Bacon?"

"What would the kids eat otherwise?"

She gave me her order, a fried egg sandwich over medium with fatty bacon and cheddar cheese.

I straightened. "Okay, well, let's do a bum scoot then and get dressed."

"What shall I wear?" she asked.

"A pair of black pants and top?" The same outfit she wore every day.

She touched her hands to her face. "I need to put on makeup."

"You look fine. Plus, we're out to catch a killer, right?" I said. "It's not a beauty contest."

* * *

When we finally reached the police station, Barbara spoke to the patrol officer at the front desk, who had the most unflattering haircut I'd ever seen. His scalp gleamed on the sides that were shaved, and then a monkish flat top crowned it off. I was sitting on a bench near the entrance where I could view the proceedings without getting involved.

"I need to speak to Sergeants Reynolds or Bronson." With Barbara's thunderous expression, neither Seth nor I would've dared mess with her.

Unfazed, he said, "Do you have an appointment?"

"That's why I'm here," Barbara said.

"You have to make an appointment."

"Now you listen here." She leaned forward and pointed a finger. "My grandchildren were threatened by one of your patrol officers, and I need to speak to somebody about that. They're involved with the case."

"We have a complaint form online."

Barbara slammed her hand on the counter, and I jumped. "I don't want to make an appointment. I want to see someone. That's why I came down here. No one returns messages."

Out of the corner of my eye, I spotted the other few people in the waiting area turning their heads. Self-conscious, my shoulders hiked up to my ears in response. This was like when Barbara picked the fight with the valet, and I'd cowered in the back seat.

The front desk officer was saying, "If you can calm down, Ma'am, I can call—who'd you say you wanted?"

"Sergeant Bronson and Sergeant Reynolds," she enunciated. Thank goodness, she'd remembered their names rather than shouting over to me.

He glanced at a screen before him, his face lighting up blue. "Okay, yeah." He picked up a phone and turned so Barbara wasn't staring him down as he spoke. When he'd finished his conversation and put down the phone, he replied to Barbara, "Yeah, just like I thought. You're going to have to call to make an appointment."

"No, I'm not." Her voice rose. "There's two women dead now, and my grandchildren have been threatened. Try the other one." He said something I couldn't hear, and she shouted, "Yeah, the man."

He repeated the phone routine, then murmured something.

"I don't want to wait," she said in the same snarl she'd used when a friend suggested that she go back to work after her husband died: *I don't want to work.* Maybe Noah had gotten some of his nastiness from her. We always tried to figure out whose side of the family was at fault.

The officer and Barbara went through the same rigmarole with the same outcome: that sergeant was unavailable, too.

I scurried back up to the front desk. "How about the lieutenant?" I said to her.

"What?!" She was so irritable now she was yelling at me, too.

"The lieutenant, the supervisor," I said.

"The lieutenant!" she boomed. "We want to see their supervisor. They might have a serial killer on their hands. We have to stop this before more women die."

"Barbara," I murmured. Now she was going overboard. Serial killers had at least three murders on their hands. We weren't to that point.

"Let me try the L.T. I thought I saw him go back to Homicide earlier." The patrol officer turned away and did more muttering into the phone. When he hung up, he said. "Okay, Lieutenant Daniels will see you. I'll need to take copies of your driver's licenses."

I didn't meet his eye as I pushed my license forward toward him.

As Barbara and I headed toward Homicide, she wanted to celebrate our victory, do a high five, but I hurried her along. The last thing I wanted was for the front desk person to see us gloating.

When we entered Homicide, a short and slight Black man with a mustache and shiny bald head greeted us. "Hello, I'm Lieutenant Daniels, head of homicide and robbery."

He took us into the conference room, where Barbara collapsed onto a chair. Broken-down printers lined the back wall. Was there nowhere else for IT to store this stuff? Someone had used the wrong kind of marker on the whiteboard at the front and had left permanent red and black writing.

I started to recount the chain of events, but once he realized how complicated it was, Lieutenant Daniels said, "Let's get Bronson and Reynolds in here, try to communicate, hear everyone out."

When he returned, he said heartily, "Okay, they're on their way. Give them about five minutes."

"Can we get a snack in the meantime? When I get this upset, my blood sugar drops." Barbara put a hand on her chest.

"My mother has diabetes, so I know how that goes." He gestured toward the door. "Please."

Sergeants Bronson and Reynolds walked in together, as if they were close friends, a few moments after we made it back to Homicide. They immediately lost their resistant edge around the lieutenant. I didn't see him as an imposing figure, but he carried the authority of rank.

He ushered us all to seats again, in the conference room. "All right, let's make sure we're operating under transparency," said Lieutenant Daniels. "Of course, we can't say much about an ongoing investigation, but our detectives work collaboratively with the families and members of the community."

Sergeant Reynolds shifted her weight, her winter jacket crackling. "We've already heard enough—"

Lieutenant Daniels cut her off. "One of the patrol officers involved in all this, maybe the responding officer, stopped this young lady in Alexandria." He indicated to me and frowned. "Let's figure out what's going on here."

"Yes, L.T.," Sergeant Bronson said. "You got it."

Sergeant Reynolds nodded, tried to press her lips into a smile. The effort was too much, and her mouth lapsed back into a pursed line.

The lieutenant put his hand on the door to leave.

"Aren't you going to stay, too?" My voice sounded rather plaintive.

He turned to his investigators. "You can handle this, right? You know I have that report to the chief due." Obviously, he couldn't wait to get out of here.

"Sure," Sergeant Bronson said.

"Can I take it from here?" I asked Barbara.

We had agreed on this; if possible, she would leave the room, and I'd handle it. She just needed to get us in, acting as pure muscle.

"Wait," she said to the lieutenant, who was about to shut the door behind him. "I'm going, too."

An expression of fright crossed his face. Even Barbara must have seen it. "Don't worry, I'm not following you."

With a nervous laugh, he bolted.

Chapter Nineteen

Week 4
Wednesday Morning

On the whiteboard at the front of the conference room was written in red marker: *Officer Camden is gay*. The two sergeants didn't seem to notice the childish slur broadcasting behind them.

Under the fluorescent lighting, Sergeant Reynolds' skin had a yellowish cast, causing her to look too old to have a newborn. "I don't know why you had to go and bring in the L.T. I thought we had a different kind of relationship." Her eye contact burned into me. I could see how she could impale suspects with that gaze.

Now she was talking about our *relationship*? After the murder in Georgetown last year, I thought we'd formed a bond. I was disappointed this time around with her lack of receptivity, chalking up the moodiness to hormones and exhaustion.

I acted as patient as I was with Alyssa when explaining a consequence. "I don't know what's happening on your end, of course. I know you're out of your mind busy. But see, on my end"—I touched a hand to my chest—"I had no idea if you planned to take under advisement anything I'd mentioned. I guess I interpreted the radio silence to mean you didn't."

Sergeant Bronson raised bloodshot eyes from his phone. "Sorry, a CI." He cleared his throat noisily. "No reason to bring in the L.T. Go ahead and talk. If there's anything, then we'll look into it." His eyes were wide and disingenuous. He was going to have to work on his poker face.

"Is it okay if I use the board?" I hopped up, sensing that, as I turned, they would exchange a look. Okay, I was used to that from my students.

I wrote Zach and Veronica as married to each other and a separate pairing of Officers Reynolds and Owen. In genogram symbolism, men were squares, women circles. When I last taught this, students objected to the gender-conforming stereotypes of "man" and "woman," as well as "husband" and "wife." This wouldn't be the same issue for the detectives behind me.

I turned. "Do you remember that story you had to read in high school, *The Gift of the Maji*, by O. Henry? The woman sells her hair to get him a watch chain, and he sells his watch to give her a comb?"

The reference landed flat. I powered on, accustomed to doing so in the face of my students' blank expressions. "Well, here, each thought the other was involved in the death." I started talking faster like a student who had to give a presentation, telling them about April Owen stopping me outside her jurisdiction and across state lines, even though D.C. wasn't a state. "She admitted that the day Emily died, she'd warned Emily to stay away from her boyfriend. It was right outside the police department where Emily was getting sick."

Sergeant Bronson's eyebrows raised.

I addressed Sergeant Reynolds. "That's why she didn't have her backpack. She didn't plan on leaving just then."

"What was wrong with her?" Sergeant Reynolds asked.

"The stress." I didn't glance over at Sergeant Bronson, who was the culprit of said stress.

"Maybe Officer Owen was trying to be nice," said Sergeant Reynolds. "Helping out a girl in trouble, offering to take her home."

"I'm sure the camera footage can tell you more. You'll see whether April forced Emily into her car and drove off." I loved a good to-do list myself, and I didn't want them to lose sight of their tasks. *Camera, p.d.* I wrote on the board.

When I turned back, I said, "Emily's autopsy found the presence of antipsychotics in her system."

Sergeant Reynolds had an air of surprise. Not that the information wasn't available to her—the medical examiner must have sent her the autopsy report, but Emily's case was a low priority.

"I think Officer Owen might have injected her with an antipsychotic, something that would knock her out."

"An injected antipsychotic—?" Sergeant Bronson was wide-eyed to Sergeant Reynolds.

"For people with schizophrenia—severe cases where noncompliance is a problem," I explained.

"Officer Owen wouldn't have access to that," he said.

"Her sister might," I replied.

"Huh?" Sergeant Bronson made an ugly face.

Sergeant Reynolds offered as explanation, "She has that sister. Every family has one."

"A black sheep?" he asked.

"Drugs," she said.

"Heroin," I added. "One of Emily's neighbors said he saw a woman in the building that resembled April's sister. I can give you his contact number."

"Wait, wait, April has a sister?" Sergeant Bronson asked.

Sergeant Reynolds and I ignored him as I explained, "She had cleaning supplies as if she was a housekeeper, but afterward, the place was still a dusty mess."

Sergeant Bronson was catching up enough to argue against my theories. "If April's sister is a heroin addict and she was at the vic's place."

He put up a beefy stop sign hand. "And I'm not saying she was, okay? Then why didn't Emily die of a heroin overdose?" he asked.

This was a question I couldn't answer. But Sergeant Reynolds did. "Because the addict wants it all to herself. She's not going to *give* it away."

I let Sergeant Bronson absorb that information, which was all the more valuable because it came from her, not me. Then I continued, "Emily was starting to find out things about Officer Randolph—his involvement with a coke dealer, how it looked like he was protecting him when it came to Siobhan's death."

Sergeant Bronson grinned, shaking his head. "You have no evidence."

"That's true. Only you can find out whether dispatch alerted Officer Randolph to a death scene or whether Officer Randolph called it in himself *after* he was already at the scene." I'd mastered writing one thing on the board and simultaneously talking about something else. In marker, I wrote *check 911 call for S* on the board, as I said, "Emily said Officer Randolph took a call on his cell right before dispatch supposedly sent a message for him to go to the scene."

I turned. "Oh, and Emily found a vial of coke among Officer Randolph's things."

"Wait, hold up." Sergeant Bronson rested his hand on his knees.

"Sergeant Reynolds knows about that already," I said.

Reynolds flashed me a sidelong glance and then turned to Sergeant Bronson. "It was found in Emily's backpack." Passive voice again. "No evidence it belonged to Officer Randolph."

I picked up my phone. "I have *evidence* of their association." Scrolling, I found the offending picture and held it up: Officer Randolph's truck parked behind Zach Naylor's place of business, *Best Barbecue*.

"Maybe he just likes barbecue," Sergeant Bronson told Sergeant Reynolds. "I like barbecue."

"One of my favorite foods," Sergeant Reynolds agreed.

"I think Zach Naylor's wife, Veronica, visited Siobhan the night of her death."

"Evidence?" asked Sergeant Reynolds sharply. Now she'd taken up the refrain.

"Siobhan was having an affair with her husband. Veronica was pregnant and would soon have three young children. There must've been something at the scene that told Zach she'd been out there—an earring, the smell of her perfume—but heck, she might've told him she was heading out there to kill his girlfriend. Check his texts." I jotted that down on the board.

"If he's a drug dealer like you say, he's going to carry burners," said Sergeant Reynolds.

"I don't know how these things work—does a dealer have one legitimate phone he uses for family and a burner for the actual dealings?" I flapped my hands to the sides. "I don't know."

The not-knowing, one-down position used in some schools of therapy worked in this case, too. To my surprise, Sergeant Reynolds said, "We can check that out easily enough."

I nodded, ensuring I stayed neutral—no need to get out before them and blow this now. I didn't even write it on the board, having decided to leave out anything that involved police officers. That would make them unnecessarily bristly. "Zach found her body. The unmarked gun might have been his. His wife knew Zach was obsessed, she saw the burn marks on his hand."

Sergeant Bronson interrupted. "Siobhan burned his hand? Then anything he did might have been self-defense."

"He burned his hand," I said, my voice hardening into what I called my *witch voice*. The children sat up a little straighter when I used it. The problem was that voice couldn't be faked. I had to be that annoyed at the tomfoolery.

"Evidence?" Sergeant Bronson said loudly.

"Have a look at his hand yourself," I suggested. "You'll see the scars."

"Self-harm is not a crime," he said.

I was impressed that he used the correct term. "I do have to warn you, Mr. and Mrs. Naylor will give each other an alibi for the night Siobhan died. She was in the Sibley ER for pregnancy complications."

"You can't be running around, committing murder when you're lying there on a gurney." Sergeant Reynolds' eyes were wide, and I remembered that she had some complications with her last pregnancy.

"Veronica's had two other kids," I said. "She knows how this works. She'd be laid up in the pelvic room for hours before being seen." I produced the written documentation from my purse that I had ready. Neither reached their hand out, so I left it on the conference table. "This is the medical record information. Of course, pulling the camera views is the only way to know who left the hospital and when." *Camera-ER*. I wrote.

"And what about the suicide note?" Sergeant Bronson was still hanging on to that.

"I have no evidence of this." I forestalled his usual line. "But I think Veronica went over there to threaten Siobhan. She might have ordered Siobhan to produce a suicide note to set up her death. Emily noticed that the note was torn from the middle of a notebook. You could try to find the journal," I suggested. "The parents might not have cleared the apartment yet. But they're working on it." I wanted to tell him *get a move on, man*, but couldn't go that far.

I walked it through with him to prevent Sergeant Bronson from going to the hypothetical future analysis of an assistant district attorney. "Veronica Naylor could probably plead pregnancy psychosis. It wasn't like she didn't have a reason to be depressed and psychotic. Her husband was a coke dealer and obsessed with a younger girlfriend. She was going to be stuck with three young children."

"So, you're saying this Zach Naylor was trying to save his wife from prison?" Sergeant Reynolds asked.

"Well, it wasn't all altruistic. If his wife was investigated, the coke business might just come out. His cop friend could only help so far."

The sergeants exchanged a glance. Then Sergeant Bronson leaned forward, and his voice lowered.

"We're going to tell you something confidential, okay? Now you can't share this or go accusing anyone. You could get someone hurt."

I folded my arms across my chest. "Okay," I said slowly, suspicious.

"Officer Randolph works undercover on the street."

"Wow," I said. This information caused me to re-examine my theories. "Under Sergeant Davids?"

"Sergeant David?" Sergeant Bronson said, clarifying the name. "We can't tell you more."

"Does Officer Owen know about her boyfriend being undercover?"

"Maybe not," Sergeant Bronson said. "The less anyone knows, the better."

"If he had such a complicated life, why would he drag my student into it?" I asked.

"She was cute. It's not that deep," said Sergeant Bronson.

* * *

Barbara was "exhausted" after we left the police department and picked up the kids, so she had to take to her bed immediately when we arrived home. I had to snag Rosa to stay with the kids and then head back to work to meet with Naomi, Lissa, Maddy, and some of the other research groups. Then I'd try to buckle down and finish a revise-and-resubmit manuscript that had languished.

Aware of Maddy's hostility, I gave them an inroad when I joined them in the computer lab. "It must've taken a long time to enter the data, huh?"

"Split between all of us, it wasn't that bad," Naomi said. "At least we had data to work with!"

"We're motivated to get this done and move on," said Maddy.

All righty, then. To that end, I assumed the "driver seat" in front of the computer with the database displayed, with the students gathered around. "First, I'm going to show you some basic descriptives. Which variables do we want to describe?" I was damned if I was going to do this for them. This *would* be a teaching moment.

"Demographics?" hazarded Lissa.

I nodded. "And which ones are those?"

"Gender, age, race/ethnicity, zip code," said Naomi.

"We tried to run them," said Maddy.

I turned to her and smiled. "Wonderful! What did you get? Do you want to show me?"

Maddy opened a folder and pulled out a stack of paper with output. Scanning the sheets, I said, "It looks like you ran the whole sample together rather than separating it by Victim Services involvement, which is what you'll want to do."

"Why don't you want the whole sample? We're studying all of them, aren't we?" Maddy spoke in a fast, snippy tone. "Can't we include it in the paper?"

I leaned back in my seat. "There's no harm in running it, but the research proposal already outlines what analysis you'll run, and the main point of your research is to look at repeat calls and compare family violence cases that involve Victim Services with those that do not. Therefore, you want to run the demographics for each and then run t-tests and chi-square analyses to make sure the two groups are comparable in their demographics."

Maddy's face hardened. "Well, we went to all that work of running it, so we want to include it in the paper."

Just like it took enormous maturity to parent children, it took a similar amount to manage students. At this point, Maddy was making even the other group members uncomfortable. They wanted to be told the correct steps rather than digging their heels in pointlessly.

"There's interesting information when you run the whole sample," she added.

"Oh? What did you find?" I asked, humoring her.

"Some of the women died," Maddy said.

"Well, a few," said Lissa.

"But haven't you said in class," asked Naomi, pushing her heavy curls back, "that some events are relatively rare, like family violence deaths?"

When I grinned at her, Naomi said, encouraged, "So even a few are important."

As I reflected on what to say, Maddy interrupted, "They didn't all die from intimate partner violence."

"No?" I *had* made that assumption.

"Some were suicides," Maddy added.

Interesting. Was this why the assistant chief stopped the research?

Naomi gave Maddy a glance. "We can't tell what the cause of death turned out to be officially. We only have the first page of the reports."

While my mind churned around this finding, I continued with the matter at hand, teaching these students. "So that's one of the 'rules,'" I air quoted. "You have to have a plan for your data analysis rather than going on a 'fishing expedition.'"

"I'm still putting it in the paper now that I've done this." Maddy chuffed an angry laugh.

I looked back at the computer screen, giving me a moment in how to deal with Maddy's obvious hostility. Fortunately, Naomi saved the day, as she often did in class. "Dr. Knight, I know you're busy, so can you show us how to run the descriptives separately by group?"

We reviewed the descriptives, then compared the two treatment conditions. At the end of that process, I said, "So now we can say that the groups are equivalent at the start and can argue that Victim Services is the crucial variable if there are differences between the conditions."

Then we moved to the fun part—to see whether involvement in services or any other variable—was associated with repeat calls. The results were generated as output right away.

"Here's the table you need." I indicated the screen. "Look at which variables are statistically significant."

"Victim Services involvement," said Lissa. "So does that mean Victim Services works?"

"Well, this number here tells you the direction of the finding." I used the cursor.

"Why is it negative?" Naomi leaned in closer.

I turned my head to include her and Lissa. Maddy was texting on her phone. I could see why people like her had made Emily feel left out of her cohort.

Focusing on the task, I said, "Can someone translate this?"

"Like if someone was involved in Victim Services, they were *more* likely to have a repeat family violence call?" Naomi plumped her hair like it helped her think.

Lissa frowned and said to Naomi, "Isn't that opposite to our hypothesis?"

"I know!" Maddy piped up, tearing her gaze from her phone. "The Victim Services counselor encouraged them to call the police if there was further violence. That's why they felt *more* comfortable calling the police. It's a good thing!"

I didn't want to seem like I was squashing her enthusiasm, so I said, "You could write that up in your discussion section to explain the findings. However, the Victim Services unit argues that its involvement means that it cuts down on calls the police have to make."

Lissa wiped her face in a gesture of exhaustion. "Wow, a lot of work to get to that point."

"That's research for you," I replied with a smile. "Email me a copy of your database, okay?"

I wanted to explore it myself. Was it a cover-up? Or something else?

Chapter Twenty

Wednesday Evening

That night, Barbara exacted her reward for playing the heavy at the police department, and we went out to Guapo's. As we waited in the restaurant for Seth to arrive after his shift ended, Alyssa simpered, perched on Barbara's leg, as Barbara stroked her hair. Barbara's legs were splayed, too wide to create a lap, and Alyssa had to hang on to her black top for balance.

Noah slumped onto the table, frowning.

"What's wrong with him?" Barbara asked.

"He didn't want to come," I said.

"Why the hell—"

"Grammy!"

She covered her mouth in *oops*. Her behavior reminded me of Sergeant Bronson's, an unwelcome comparison.

"He wanted to stay at home." I sipped my water, trying to remain calm. When he was home he acted out, making it impossible for everyone else. On the other hand, he didn't like to leave home, either.

"You love Guapo's!" Barbara said to him.

It was Noah's favorite restaurant, despite the number of times he'd been walked outside, crying, while I stared longingly at my plate of enchiladas *verde* through the window. As the cheese congealed, I would lament Guapo's no-microwave policy.

Noah took his pacifier out and said, "When are we going home?" That was always a clear sentence, one he said often.

I offered my arms, and he gladly clambered into my lap, sucking harder on his pacifier. I asked Barbara, "Do you think you could get us back into the police department?"

"Again?"

I told her my new theory.

She sighed. "You just got done convincing those detectives to look into that horrible man." Barbara hadn't forgiven Zach Naylor for his remarks about her. "And his barbecue wasn't even that good."

"All fat," I agreed. "But my students re-entered the data that Emily had in hard copy reports. Some of the women who were in a certain sector, which included both Emily and the other young woman who died, also died in the year following the call. We couldn't tell what those deaths were ruled as or much information about the initial family violence call because Emily only printed down the front pages of the reports. As it was, it was a lot of data to weed through."

Barbara lost interest in my explanation as the chips arrived with four bowls of salsa.

Relieved to see Seth walk in the door, I waved frantically at him to join us.

* * *

The following day after drop off, Barbara and I headed to the Metro police department. I let Barbara out in front at her command as horns blared behind me. I winced.

The only spot I could find was a ten-minute walk, and when I entered the police department, I spotted Barbara on a bench in the waiting area.

I eyed her curiously as I came up. "What did they say?"

"I was just taking a little rest. I haven't been up to the desk yet."

"What's the plan?" She'd bragged she could get us in again, "easy peasy."

She swatted my question away.

"Shall I just go to the desk and ask for Ethan?" I asked.

"No!" She scowled. "We need to surprise him."

I sat beside her, my crossed leg bouncing as we watched the goings-on at the desk. A different officer was at the front today. I was glad since Officer Flat-Top would remember the obnoxious grandmother and her nervous daughter-in-law sidekick.

Finally, Barbara said, "Come on, help me up. I can say I need the restroom or have a low blood sugar attack."

I did the two-handed heave-ho to get Barbara to her feet. We started the slow, snail-like process to the desk area, and then we got lucky. We were moving at such a pace that, in the meantime, an entire extended family flocked in and mobbed the desk with their myriad members.

I sped up, leaving Barbara behind, afraid an authoritative voice would call out, "Ma'am, can I help you?" When I arrived at the elevator bank, I waited around in agitation until Barbara caught up.

Breathing hard, Barbara stabbed a taupe-colored fingernail at the elevator button, even though I'd already pushed it. When it arrived, she ordered, "Get in!" There, she poked at the button for the fourth floor. The elevator remained in place.

"See, we need to have a pass," I said. With that, the elevator light switched to *down*.

"I guess we're going to the basement first," Barbara said. "Well, while we're here, I might as well get a little snack." Her crankiness faded, and she smiled in anticipation.

We did the vending machine thing again, and thus, laden with chips and another Diet Coke, we clambered back into the elevator, which automatically took us back up to the ground floor.

This time, Barbara's *chutzpah* paid off. The dispatcher with the cane, wearing a puffy vest over the regulation polyester uniform, appeared at the bank of elevators. I held it open as she made her way in.

"I really think it's great what you guys do," Barbara said.

The dispatcher waved her badge at the fourth floor.

"Oh, thank you." The dispatcher turned to smile at us. She wore an early nineties curly perm with straight-across thick bangs.

Barbara gave me a little punch of triumph in the arm. I had assumed the dispatcher was older because of the cane, but when I looked into her face, I realized she was about my own age. "You've been up here before," she said. "My name is Donna Claflin."

I grinned, grateful toward her for getting us access. "I'm Cara, and this is my mother-in-law, Barbara."

Donna chattered about how long she'd worked there—fifteen years—and how she liked everything about it, except for the shift work. I had just read a study that concluded that people on those schedules were more likely to suffer from anxiety and depression. But her affect seemed pretty bright. When we landed on four, Donna had to weave around Barbara, who blocked the hallway. I apologized profusely as Barbara waved her ahead.

"Sorry, gotta punch in on time," the dispatcher said.

When the woman made the next turn, Barbara gasped. "I need to sit down."

I touched her arm to encourage some movement. "We've got just a little further, and then I'm sure I can find you a seat." In all fairness to Barbara, she'd probably walked more this week than she had the month before in Miami.

Just as I thought we were making progress, she stopped and pulled out a bag of chips from her purse. "My blood sugar's low." After some fumbling, she jammed a couple of chips in her mouth before offering me the bag.

Shaking my head, I decided to go ahead to Ethan's cubicle and see if he had an extra chair.

At his office, I noticed that his computer and desk light were on. Hopefully, that meant he was in the station somewhere and would be back soon. Hearing Barbara panting behind me, I moved aside to get out of her way.

"I'm just going to sit here." She staggered toward Ethan's chair, the only one in the cubicle. She dropped down so heavily, she was lucky not to have gone ass-over-teakettle off the back.

"You can't do that!" As cheeky as students were now, I'd never caught one of them behind my desk, although one had dragged her desk in front of mine facing the other students.

Ethan suddenly came up behind me, and I yelped in surprise. His focus was on Barbara. "What are you doing in my chair?"

"I tried to tell her," I murmured.

Unconcerned, she fished in the bag for another chip.

"Look, we can make this quick," I said. "And then you can have your seat."

"Who's she?" he asked, still fixated.

"I wanted to talk to you about the family violence data," I said.

He ducked his head and lowered his voice. "Hey, I already told you what happened."

"I know, Assistant Chief, Jim LeFevre." I made it a statement rather than a question so that he would reveal more.

His eyes widening, he reared back.

Bingo, I'd gotten the name right. Ethan would have to work on his poker face.

I continued to box him in. "LeFevre used to be lieutenant of family violence before his promotion to assistant chief. He knew the death rates for women who called the police for family violence was higher than over previous years. He was more interested in covering it up than trying to find out why. That was just fine with you, wasn't it? You have access to all this data. Did you use it to find women to target?"

He folded short arms against an undeveloped chest and scoffed. "What are you accusing me of? This is crazy."

Barbara fished in her purse for the Diet Coke and held it out to me. "Would you open this? I don't want to break a nail, and I won't be able to get another appointment until I'm back."

I loosened the cap and handed it back to her, still talking to Ethan. "Since you wouldn't mesh the databases for her, Emily printed out all the records from two years ago and matched the victim names to the following year. I have a list in my purse of the women who died, but two of them were Emily Vinter and Siobhan Weaver."

"We're not supposed to print out that much now that we've gone green," he said.

"That's the least of your worries, and you know it."

Barbara munched on her chips, entertained by our exchange.

He leaned over and scooped up his phone. "If you don't leave now, I'll call the front desk and have you escorted out."

To Barbara, I said, straining for nonchalance. "Let's go down to Homicide and talk to the lieutenant there." This was a total bluff, of course. The other day, I'd just gone out on a limb by moving up the chain of command to have Sergeants Bronson and Reynolds pay attention to my theories about Zach Naylor, his wife, and Officers Randolph and Owen. I could imagine the eye rolls if I suddenly raised suspicions in a completely different direction.

Ethan pushed buttons on his phone. "Yeah, this is Ethan Banks from the fourth floor—"

"Come on, Barbara, let's go." I was a married mother of two young children and a college professor, for heaven's sake. I wasn't someone who had to be forcibly removed by police officers. And what if Dean Bingham found out?

Of course, there was no way to perform a graceful or speedy exit around her. I had to help her out of the chair as Ethan said into his phone, "I have two women in my office who don't have passes. Someone needs to come up here and escort them out."

'Okay, okay, we're leaving," I said, genuinely alarmed now. "Come on, Barbara."

With phone to ear, Ethan said, "Okay, it looks like they're going. They should be downstairs in a minute."

Of course, it would take more than that with Barbara. I could barely control my agitation at almost being thrown out of the police department. That was before I spotted the desk sergeant standing and frowning our way.

When we finally strolled past the front desk, the officer with the flat top was there and grumbled, "You two again."

It would have been so much better to actually speak in person to one of the homicide investigators or the lieutenant, but we were no longer welcome today. After we'd driven back to Virginia, the best I could do was to leave voicemail messages about my new concerns. I even named all the women who had supposedly died from suicide, cross-referencing from the student database and the hard copy cases. I didn't know what had happened in these cases because we only had the first page of the reports, but I wondered if the circumstances were like Siobhan's, where there was arguing but no violence, and an arrest wasn't warranted. But did I think the police would listen to yet another theory? No. I had cried wolf too many times.

Chapter Twenty-One

Thursday Evening

To cap the day, I had to teach my night section of research. The student attitude was negative. They were tired, no one wanted to be there, and it was late when we finished, even though I let them go ten minutes early at nine-thirty.

After last year's attack, I'd been requiring the students to walk out as a group. I wasn't about to enforce the policy tonight and plead with them to wait for me. I left quickly, going straight to my office and dropping my books and papers before grabbing my bag and coat.

I was almost to the double doors that led into the main hallway when I heard a desk scraping against the floor in the multi-purpose classroom. Startled, I turned. A man with pale, nondescript features and thinning, mouse-brown hair, about fifteen years older than the students, strolled out.

A cold wash of fear sharpened my mind. He was the partner of the disabled dispatcher, Donna. The first time I'd seen him, he'd pushed Donna up to the fourth floor in a wheelchair. But there had been a second time. On Siobhan Weaver's street, when Barbara and I'd posed as apartment hunters, I'd passed this man in the intersection. He'd worn a hat and scarf. Was he trying to disguise himself? Or was he doing business in the neighborhood where he lived, and two other women had been killed?

I lunged for the door handle. I was in danger now, too.

Right now, safe at home, Barbara was on her nighttime routine, taking a Klonopin after a shower, putting on lotions, unaware of the danger I was in. Seth was likely watching the news. He'd probably already walked the kids up the stairs and, standing in the hallway between their two rooms, was saying, *good night*, at this very moment.

Noah would've asked, *Where's Mom?*

The heart-wrenching fear of leaving my babies motherless made me lunge for the door handle.

"Don't move!" The man snarled and jammed the barrel of a gun into my spine.

My hand fell.

"Turn around, then drop your bags," he ordered.

I dropped my purse and briefcase, which landed on the floor with an eerie thud, before turning to face the culprit who had taken the lives of Emily and Siobhan.

"Change positions with me. And don't even try for the door again." Spittle hit the side of my neck as he pushed to his other side, the gun firmly pressed against my shirt. He leaned over and punched the button lock, so no one could come in from the outside.

This was my only chance to take advantage of his momentary distraction, and I bolted in the only direction I could, down the hallway, weaving and praying he didn't shoot.

"You can't get out that way. There's no use," he shouted behind me.

He'd obviously staked out the space. Maybe he wouldn't bother shooting me if he thought I was trapped. As I ran, I calculated my odds. If he did decide to shoot, he'd have to take a moment to get into position, giving me time . . . I ran as fast as my boots would allow.

I hurtled down the three steps that led to the lower level and the faculty offices and ripped open the door to the electric room on the left.

BOOM! A noise like a canon echoed down the hallway. A fearsome whine from the force of the shot rang through my eardrums. Glass from the faculty office walls shattered.

I slammed the door behind me. The button lock would be easy to break, but at least it would put a barrier between me and this madman.

With all the shooting, surely someone would hear?

But no one was in the building this late. I despaired.

As a stalling technique, I grabbed a broken chair and rolled it on its lopsided wheels toward the door. Orienting myself toward the recycling bins, I flicked off the light and headed over to them. Grasping with my hands, I found the lid and pushed it up, forcing it to slam closed. I hoped he would hear as I tiptoed off.

The gun butt banging against the metal door made me jump, then stumble into a set of cardboard boxes like Jenga blocks that tumbled to the floor.

A deafening shot rang out.

I hit the floor instinctively, crashing into more boxes.

The man jimmied the lock, and the whole knob apparatus clanked onto the tile floor of the hallway, leaving an echoing ring in the air. He pushed the door open, and light oozed in.

I remained still, breathing quietly through my nose the pulp smell of cardboard surrounding me.

He crashed, swearing, into the chair I'd planted. The wheels rattled unevenly until they rolled to a stop.

"You're very clever, Miss Professor, but not as smart as me." His voice was calm, like he was enjoying this game of cat and mouse.

He seemed to be orienting himself to the room, and his voice sounded again. "Did you wonder how I found the women that the police couldn't help?" He chuckled softly, an eerie sound. "I have the police band app."

He seemed to want to talk, show off his cleverness.

But he was only telling me because he was intent on my not surviving.

"I'd wander down to the scene, get a look, see if the woman was young and attractive. They allow men to be violent with them. They must want it."

Nausea balled at the back of my throat at his sick rationalizations.

A nail pinged across the room as his feet scuffed the floor. "Donna wanted me to work." Resentment seeped into his tone. "So, I told her, hey, I freelance. One of these days, I'll go to a scene and get a photo of a politician, a TV newscaster, or some local celebrity being led out for domestic violence."

His voice grew further away, and I wondered if my second gambit would pay off. "Do you know how much the news outlets would pay?"

That was how he justified being out at all hours? The monologue was turning into a case study on delusion, problems with authority, entitlement, and unemployment.

In the dark and in my fear, his voice seemed to be facing the other direction. "Donna said I was unlike other men. I listened." He chuckled ominously, and a cold, electric shiver of terror tore through my body.

Meanwhile, he must've used her—for financial support and her specialized knowledge of police procedure and operations.

"The night I met Siobhan . . ." The way he said it was sickening, like it was a romantic encounter. "The police dispatched Victim Services and the young lady who showed up was almost as pretty as Siobhan."

The roar in the room resounded in my chest like the planes flying over Gravely Point on their way to Reagan Airport. Gunfire. He'd followed my misleading breadcrumbs to the bin and shot inside, thinking I was there.

I lunged for the hidden exit door, cardboard knocking around me. I tripped on the uneven ground and stumbled, caught myself with my hands on the cement. Pain sliced through my index finger, and I wondered if it was broken glass. The whine of the shots had faded. It was so quiet I feared moving and giving away my position. My finger was throbbing, and I could feel blood seeping from the cut. My hands scraped against the brick wall as I desperately sought out the doorknob to the exit on this side of the building. I envisioned him peering into the bin with his makeshift flashlight, and not finding my dead body inside. *Can't pass me off as a suicide, pal!*

He roared at the discovery. My moment of triumph was short-lived when a light shone on the wall above me. He was coming this way, and he could see me.

I dove at the door, running into the piece of glass again with my foot.

"I've got you now," he crowed. "Turn around and put your hands on your head."

I heard the catch of the gun as I leaned over and picked up the glass. I sliced my fingers again, but that only made me aware of the jagged edge, which I hurled at him like a frisbee.

As he screamed, I fumbled for the doorknob and charged out into the brightly lit fluorescent hallway of the job training center next door.

I bolted down the hallway to the door to the main foyer of the building. Behind me, the door from the electric room swung open. Before he could emerge, I hurried out into the main building hallway and sprinted to the double glass doors at the entrance.

As he fired again, more glass shattered. I tore open the door and once outside, I swiveled around in the cold air. My choices: exposure in the parking lot lights; or the bushes and shadow of the building.

Smoot Lumber. I ran for my life to the open truck bay. "Help!"

Chapter Twenty-Two

Week 5
Monday Morning

My near death was finally justification for Sergeants Bronson and Reynolds to coordinate their cases. Better late than never! They requested I come down to the station for my "official" statement the following Monday morning, even though I'd told my story to various law enforcement officials, including them, until nearly dawn Friday morning. I returned home from the ordeal just in time for Noah to wake up with the sun.

When I walked into the Homicide conference room, Sergeant Reynolds was seated with a laptop in front of her ready to be the official scribe. "Don't be thinking you can keep doing this," she said to me.

"Yeah," Sergeant Bronson reiterated, standing, as if too excited to sit. "You got lucky this once."

"Ahem, twice," I clarified, indicating Sergeant Reynolds and my history on the last case.

Bronson glanced over at Sergeant Reynolds, who gave a curt nod. He raised his eyebrows and said, "Damn."

I sat at the conference table. "So, I'm coming down here voluntarily to give another detailed statement, and I've assisted the case in every way possible. I gave you the database the students constructed, and the hard copy files of the cases, which have the identity of the victims. So, your task force—" I looked up at Sergeant Bronson, who had his hands on hips revealing his sidearm under the jacket. "Can now cross-reference the follow-up calls to supposed overdoses, suicides, and accidental death of women involved in previous domestic disputes." Sergeant Bronson well knew that I'd offered him dibs on the data, pointing out his possession of it would make him logical head of the task force. He had thus wrested control from Fairfax County, where Martin Scott's attack on me had occurred.

"So, it's only fair," I said in a reasonable tone, "that you agree to a couple of things, too."

Sergeant Reynolds stirred restlessly in her chair as if I had elicited her inner big cat, and Bronson took a few steps toward the whiteboard. He pointed at it, as if my statement would be posted there. "Let's get on with it."

I sat down and started with Assistant Chief LeFevre's role. "He knew of the increased death rates of young women among the family violence and disturbance cases and didn't want that fact to come to light."

In response, the sergeants assumed their typical blank expressions with hard eye contact. To penetrate their professional mask, I asked, "What do you plan to do with this information?"

"We'll talk to the L.T., see what he says," Bronson said off-handedly.

"I don't want to go to the *Post*." I waited to see if they'd take the bait, but they held their silence. "But I will if nothing comes of it."

"We'll look into it," Sergeant Reynolds replied testily. "Now we need to finish this here statement."

Taking her promise at face value, I continued. "Ethan, the IT guy, and I went back and forth a few times about the research, and, at one point . . ." I gave an embarrassed chuckle. "I thought he was the perpetrator, and that he'd blocked the research to avoid being found out that he was using the data to troll for potential victims. But he was acting on Assistant Chief LeFevre's orders. His cubicle, as you know, is right near the dispatchers, and they can hear his conversations when they go by. According to Martin Scott, his girlfriend Donna told him everything. And that's one thing I'd like to know—what was her level of involvement?"

I was startled when Sergeant Bronson stomped to the end of the room. I realized it was from excitement when he crowed, "Oh, her ass has been fired!"

"Did she know?"

Sergeant Bronson rolled his eyes. "You know what they say—you can't fix stupid."

What was the moral of the story: If a man listened well, he was not to be trusted and just might even be a serial killer.

Reynolds looked up over her screen. "At the very least, she provided the suspect with confidential information about procedure."

As Bronson paced back to where he'd been standing, he said, "She'll be lucky not to be charged with a serious crime. You ask me, she's lucky to be alive at all. He pressured her into a life insurance policy, with him as sole beneficiary." He grinned and shook his head, and I wondered why he was looking so pleased when I had brought him the case wrapped up in a bow, albeit with a dozen stitches to show for it.

I'd bled a trail all the way from the next-door suite, into the lobby, and to the garage at Smoot Lumber. But, all in all, I was lucky. When I whipped that broken glass plate at Martin Scott, it caught him on the trigger hand, slicing a tendon and requiring surgery.

"I know how to get serial killers to talk," he said, all but flexing.

"What did he tell you that we didn't know?" I asked.

Sergeant Reynolds raised her head and was about to shut it down, but Sergeant Bronson spouted off before she had the chance. "Our suspect wasn't the only person there that night. At about midnight, a black BMW pulled up. Our serial killer recognized the car from other 'occasions.'" I'd never seen him this cheerful. Serial killers apparently boosted his mood. "The suspect believed it to be Vic One's boyfriend."

"Zach Naylor," I supplied.

He pointed at me. "Instead, it was Naylor's wife, Veronica. She just found evidence of his affair with Siobhan, including keys to her place."

"So, Veronica lets herself in to confront Siobhan," I said.

"And waves a six-millimeter around." Involuntarily, Sergeant Bronson touched his own sidearm.

"That was the unlicensed gun?" I suspected that Officer Randolph had given the weapon to Zach Naylor—street officers ran into a lot of unlicensed guns, and their owners preferred if the officer just took it rather than pressing charges. But it wasn't time to bring that up.

Sergeant Bronson nodded shortly, confirming my suspicions that it was a touchy subject, and went on. "So, Naylor's wife and the victim struggle over the gun, and it goes off."

I glanced at Sergeant Reynolds to see how she was receiving all this. She was reading something on her screen and not paying attention to his storytelling. I, meanwhile, was a rapt audience, and Sergeant Bronson knew it.

"Zach Naylor, seeing the text messages from his wife that she's going to kill his mistress, heads over there. He arrives too late. His girlfriend is dead."

When he paused, I guessed, "So he thinks his wife did it and tries to cover for her."

"He read his girlfriend's diary before, poor guy. All sorts of suicidal shit in there. Easy to rip any page out. A ready-made note."

Although I was too big a person to point out that I'd outlined this theory before I was attacked, I couldn't resist saying, "And then Zach Naylor called Officer Randolph to fix it. As the responding officer, he influenced how the scene was interpreted."

I kept my language in the passive voice to avoid Sergeant Bronson getting his hackles up, but it was Sergeant Reynolds, not looking up from her screen, who said, "We can't talk about what Officer Randolph did or didn't do given his assignment."

At this point, I thought the alleged "assignment" either bull hockey or Officer Randolph had gone to the dark side soon after receiving it. I would look forward to news of *his* firing also, which was the least he deserved after leading Emily to her death.

"So as Veronica Naylor fled the scene," I said. "Martin Scott posed as a tenant and got in. He was waiting for his chance." I had my hand to my mouth, seeing how the night unfolded. "Emily caught his eye the night she counseled Siobhan Weaver. After he killed Siobhan, he heard from his girlfriend the scuttlebutt that Emily had confronted you." I pointed to Sergeant Bronson.

Mrs. Vinter had imagined someone stalking Emily, and she'd turned out to be right. The Vinters might have a civil case against the landlord for not providing the window coverings after all.

"My question is, how did Emily get from here to her apartment that day?" I asked.

Sergeant Bronson folded his hands, leaning against the table. "We're checking Ubers, taxis, metro, bus. We'll figure it out."

Used to silent and non-receptive audiences in research, I forged on. "April Owen was jealous, rightfully so—her boyfriend was gallivanting with a pretty, young intern. Instead of taking it up with her partner, she blamed the affair on Emily." I expected the sergeants' blank faces. They would always have to side with the police officer in the story. "April has a sister that struggles with addiction. She might have been desperate enough to do April a favor." The sergeants didn't blink when I met their eyes. "That day, Emily must have been texting Jack

Randolph, distraught because she was about to be dismissed. April might have intercepted the messages."

Sergeant Reynolds shifted and murmured, "You don't know that."

I nodded acknowledgment but continued the scenario. "April's sister was driving April's black Explorer, and Emily was ill outside on the street. Rendered weak and woozy, Emily must have been easy to manipulate into the car, especially if April's sister promised to drop Emily at her apartment."

Sergeant Reynolds pursed her lips in disparagement.

"I'm not sure how far April wanted her sister to take it," I admitted. "Was it to scare Emily, or her boyfriend?"

I peered at Sergeants Reynolds and Bronson as if they had the answer. When they didn't speak, I said, "April was kidding herself if she didn't think her sister would take the heroin that was supposed to make Emily look like an overdose. Here it's really conjecture—"

Her eyes trained back on the screen, Reynolds replied, "And the rest isn't?"

I shrugged. "It's not unheard of that people with substance use disorders have a co-occurring mental illness."

"A what?" asked Sergeant Bronson.

"Many people use drugs to cope with an underlying disorder. April's sister might have been diagnosed with schizophrenia or schizoaffective disorder at some point, and maybe court-ordered to get an injectable antipsychotic."

I wondered if April's sister showed some borderline personality behaviors, like seducing a tech who was going to administer the shot at an outpatient clinic?

"I know I'm going out on a limb here." I opened my hands on the table to show I had nothing to hide. "The antipsychotic was probably Haldol. It's old school and pretty tough to tolerate. With a big enough dose, Emily might've been sedated or at least disoriented." I knew that Washington D.C. public clinics used first-generation antipsychotics over the second-generation ones because of cost. "This can all be confirmed."

"You like to put people to work, don't you?" Sergeant Reynolds remarked.

I chuckled. "My administrative assistant says that, too."

Sergeant Bronson folded his arms across his distended chest. "Now you're saying April Owens did it. No, no way. I got him to confess. Even the FBI can't always get these mothers to do that."

"What I'm saying is, like the last time, Martin Scott did so much planning and stalking, he could seize on the moment. At some point, April's sister abandoned the project, either having done the job her sister assigned her or whether a premature departure was due to her own need for drugs. Martin Scott took over to finish the job. He struck Emily in the temple with a blunt object to render her unconscious, then turned on the burners, and positioned her body so that the coffee table nearby could explain the bruise." I swallowed the shock of discovering Emily's body and the sadness bubbling up. At least her parents would be consoled that their daughter had not done this to herself and would be justified if they decided to bring suit.

Sergeant Reynolds sighed. "Okay, I finished your statement. I left out the supposition and the hearsay. I sent it to the printer. I'll grab it and you can review and sign it."

Once I had her abbreviated version, I scanned it quickly for content rather than correct grammatical errors. Focusing on the big picture, like with my student papers.

Chapter Twenty-Three

Monday Evening

Barbara, Seth, the kids, and I were out to celebrate the end of the case with another dinner at Guapo's. "Seth, I think we need a toast," Barbara held up her glass, beaming. She took such pride in her son's toasts.

Seth and I held our water glasses up. Barbara swished her Diet Coke, and the kids had their 7UP. "To Mom," Seth cheered. "She's so smart she solved a case the police didn't even know about."

The kids were most delighted about being able to clink cups, even though they had plastic ones with lids, and we did that for a while until Alyssa dropped hers and 7UP slopped all over the table.

Seth wrapped his arm around me as we munched on chips and queso, overprotective after my near-death experience.

"I wish you'd have called *me*," Barbara said.

"You were asleep," She also wouldn't have heard the phone if I had called.

"I was just lying there. My Klonopin didn't even work that night. I must've sensed something was wrong."

Seth rolled his eyes toward me. Barbara was always trying to take credit.

"If it wasn't for me," she continued, "you wouldn't have entered the police department to confront that IT person. I was the one who set everything into motion." She grinned.

"You're right, Barbara. You played a critical role. I'm glad you came up instead of attending that rice program in North Carolina."

"And I was the first person to think he was a serial killer."

I must've given a quizzical face, not quite remembering it that way.

The busser delivered two bowls of chips and salsa with a flourish. Seth and I kept one to ourselves that didn't get pawed through, over-salted, and double-dipped, and we left the other to Barbara and the kids.

Barbara continued, "Remember when I was yelling at that front desk police man with that terrible haircut? I said we might be facing a serial killer then."

"But, Mom, didn't you just say that for effect, so he would take you seriously?" Seth asked and scooped up salsa with a chip.

"No, I really thought that," she said, her eyes wide and earnest.

Seth chomped down on the chip a little harder than necessary. Usually, I was the one more annoyed with her, but I was still glad to be alive, making me less irritable than usual. Still insulted by Zach's comments, my mother-in-law asked, "And that bad man is going to go to jail?"

"The Metro P.D. was pretty cagey about anything to do with their Narcotics unit and Officer Randolph, but the FBI is interested." The serial killer case intersected with the pill-pushing Dr. Leven. He had died of a heart attack, likely cocaine induced. The FBI could trace where he'd operated and who else was involved. Certainly, Zach Naylor, who had a business arrangement with Dr. Leven. And, of course, the FBI would want to develop a profile of Martin Scott. If I had to guess, I would suggest that his mother had suffered abuse from various partners and then possibly ended her own life, or her perpetrator had killed her and covered it up with a staged suicide. Martin re-enacted the scene, finding young women who their partners had abused and then killing them, making it look like suicide.

Barbara preened. "What are we going to do next?"

Seth answered for me. "We're just going to have a nice quiet visit, and then you're going back to Miami to rest after all the excitement."

"What does that turkey in Richmond have to say about all this?" she asked, eyebrows dancing.

I chuckled at her calling Dean Bingham a turkey. "I'm sure he'll use it as one more reason to shut down the campus."

"It wasn't your fault a homicidal maniac attacked you," she replied.

I glanced at the kids. Shielded from all the talk of violence, they were giggling, sugar high from their sodas, and not paying attention.

"He should be happy you're bringing such positive attention to the school." She licked salt off her fingers. "All that free publicity."

"You'd think so." I nibbled on a chip as I considered. "If I didn't know him better, I'd think he was jealous."

"Of course, he's jealous," said Seth. "Although any attention for a professor increases the school's reputation, he doesn't want anyone getting more attention than him."

We stopped talking as the waiters arrived with large trays balanced on one upraised hand and unloaded steaming plates onto the table.

The prospect of the off-campus closing was a problem for another day. My little world was safe again. We dug into our celebratory dinner. I'd solved a serial killer case and brought attention to a drug-dealing ring. Nearing springtime, the dark, cold days of winter would soon be behind us.

About the Author

Jacque Rosman (Jacqueline Corcoran) lives outside Washington D.C. with her husband, two children, two cats, and a rescue chihuahua. She is the author of *A Surrealist Affair*. *Murder In Georgetown* is the first in the Academic Mom Mystery Series.

Upcoming New Release!

JACQUE ROSMAN'S

Murder at the Waterfront
The Academic Mom Mystery Series
Book Three

Cara Knight supervises a student at the Washington D.C. Grief and Loss Center which provides counselor accompaniment of relatives of the deceased to the downtown morgue. When Cara's student complains about the unfair treatment his African-American clients suffer, with their families' bodies often languishing for months until the autopsy is complete, she reminds him of the social work mandate to change the system.

What she didn't have in mind is his angry confrontation of the chief medical examiner, Sanford Mullen, after which Mullen is found dead, stacked on top of other bodies and a victim of his own scalpel...

For more information
visit: www.SpeakingVolumes.us

Now Available!

JACQUE ROSMAN

Murder in Georgetown
The Academic Mom Mystery Series
Book One

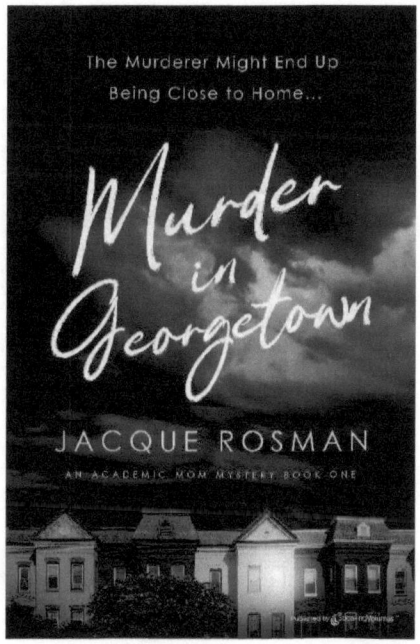

**For more information
visit: www.SpeakingVolumes.us**

Now Available!

ANNE SHAW HEINRICH

God Bless the Child
The Women of Paradise County
Book One

For more information
visit: www.SpeakingVolumes.us

Now Available!

GERI SPIELER

Regina of Warsaw
Book One

Winner of the 2024 New York Book Festival Award

Inspired by Real Events

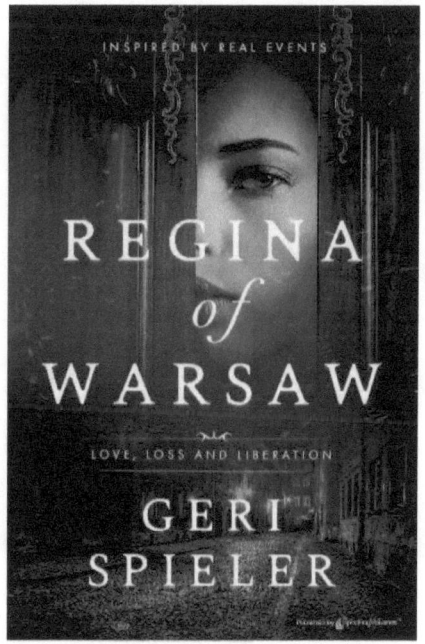

For more information
visit: www.SpeakingVolumes.us

Now Available!

CHARLENE WEXLER

Murder on Skid Row

For more information
visit: www.SpeakingVolumes.us

www.ingramcontent.com/pod-product-compliance
Lightning Source LLC
LaVergne TN
LVHW041701070526
838199LV00045B/1148